THE NIGHT BEFORE

A SEATTLE SASQUATCH NOVEL

HARPER ROBSON

2023

E Book Cover by Cate Ashwood. Ashwood Designs

Paperback Cover by Cate Ashwood and 100 Covers

Edited by Sandra and Julia at One Love Editing

Contents

Before We Get Started

A Note From Harper

One of the side characters in *The Night Before* comes from an abusive childhood and was emancipated from her parents when she was a teenager. It is described briefly on page.

There is also a character who suffers from dementia and is in a care home. There is a brief incident where this character slaps someone.

CTE

Dr. Ben Jacobs, one of the main characters in *The Night Before*, is a researcher who studies CTE, which stands for *chronic traumatic encephalopathy*. This condition is thought to be linked to repeated head injuries or blows to the head, which can damage the brain.

If you would like to learn more about the condition, please check out the Boston University CTE Center at https://www.bu.edu/cte/

I've done my best to represent dementia patients as sensitively and accurately as possible, so please forgive any errors.

Thanks so much for reading and I hope you enjoy Aleks & Ben's story!

CHAPTER 1
Ben

"Yikes," I mutter under my breath as I get out of my warm car into the cold wind and rain of late autumn in Seattle. It's still dark at this early hour, but even after the sun rises, this promises to be one of those days that make transplants to the Pacific Northwest break down and cry.

After locking my car, I hustle across the wet parking lot into the hospital wing that houses my office, as well as the few patients I'm currently treating. I spend most of my time these days on research, studying traumatic brain injuries, specifically CTE, which is the condition that can result when someone gets hit in the head a lot, people like athletes and military folks. Researching ways to keep people safe from preventable brain injuries is my passion, and I've spent the last couple of years working with a talented team of researchers, engineers and other smart people to come up with a new type of hockey helmet. I still love working with real people though, so I always have a couple of surgical patients under my care.

"Morning, Nadia," I call to the nurse on duty, who gives me a bright smile.

"Hey, Dr. Benny. Go stash your coat and bag. I'll do you a solid and grab your coffee for you. It's too damn cold and wet out there to go without it this morning," she says, sliding out of her chair and heading down the hall toward the small coffee station. The ward is dark and things are still quiet, making this my favorite time of day. Visitors and families haven't arrived and most other docs don't come in to do their rounds until later, so it's just the nursing staff, the patients and me.

After hanging my coat in the small staff room, I find Nadia back at the nurses' station which is adorably decorated for the holidays. Colorful string lights are attached to the edges of the counter, along with red, green, and gold ribbon. On one corner of the counter is a tiny Christmas tree decorated with mini surgical instruments and sterile gloves, strips of gauze as garland. It sparkles with blue and white LED lights, and at the top sits a sparkly silver star. In various doorways are mistletoe sprigs hung with red velvet ribbons, and on one wall, a beautiful miniature quilt is displayed featuring the Star of David and a menorah, which was gifted to us one year during Hannukah.

"The place looks amazing, Nadi," I comment as she hands me a steaming mug of motivation.

"Thanks. I'm happy with it. You know I love doing that kind of shit." She grins.

I chuckle. "You're always trying to make everyone think you're this total hard-ass, but I know the softie that lurks underneath."

She winks at me and hands me a tablet containing the chart updates for my patients.

"How did things go last night?" I ask with a grateful smile as I take that perfect first sip. The tension in my shoulders releases a little as the caffeine hits my bloodstream.

"Very quiet, just the way we like it." She smiles. "You'll see it in the notes, but Mr. McHanna had his best night since surgery."

"Thank god for that," I say, good news about one of my favorite patients relaxing me further. "If he continues in that direction, maybe we can discharge him by the weekend, and his daughter can help him get settled at home," I mutter half to myself as I glance over the detailed notes.

Nadia gives me a fond look, her big brown eyes crinkling up at the corners. "You know, Ben, you are the only doc I know who always remembers whether patients have help at home. It's nice. The others all leave those pesky details to the social workers."

Heat rises in my cheeks, and her smile turns mischievous. "Now, don't go getting all embarrassed," she says. "I just want you to know we appreciate you, that's all."

"Oh, you know, it's really only because I have fewer patients than the other docs—" I start to protest, but she waves her hand and gives me a dirty look over the rims of her bright pink glasses.

"Benjamin Jacobs, you need to take a compliment when someone gives it to you." The look on her face is stern, but she softens it by shooting me a wink.

"Now, then," she continues. "We both know I'm speaking the truth, buuuut... I do have a favor to ask you..." From the look on her face, I get the feeling I might not like what's coming next.

I roll my eyes. "Ahh, now the truth comes out. Were you just buttering me up for something?"

She laughs. "Of course not—you know I'd never lie to you! But I *did* think it might not hurt to remind you of how amazing you are before asking you for a small favor..." She looks a little sheepish.

I give her the "hurry up" motion with my hands. "Alright, spit it out, then."

"Well," she begins. "I just got a panicked call from my sister, Irena. Dr. Madsen had to cancel his speech for tomorrow night." She pauses, and suddenly, I know exactly where this is going.

"Oh noooo..." I groan.

Nadia's sister, Irena, works for a nonprofit that supports research into brain and spinal cord injury, and their biggest fundraiser of the year is this weekend. It's a big, fancy gala, raising huge amounts of money from Seattle's wealthy and kicking off the holiday fundraising season. Their keynote speaker for this year is a prestigious researcher who also happens to be my old professor and friend, Dennis Madsen. His lab at Boston University is the world's preeminent center for studying brain injuries, and my dream is to take over that lab and continue his research one day. I'm hopeful our newly developed helmet will help convince both him and his university that I'm the right candidate for his job, whenever he's ready to retire.

"His wife had some kind of medical emergency," Nadia continues. "But he recommended you as someone who could easily give the keynote address in his place."

I'd been looking forward to catching up with Dr. Madsen at the gala this weekend. Our research team just finished negotiating a deal with Seattle's new NHL team, the Sasquatch, to wear our helmets for a series of games around their Christmas break. The incredible tech embedded in the helmets records real-time data about how the brain reacts when players get hit. Dr. Madsen has been super supportive, and I've been wanting to update him, so I'm selfishly disappointed he won't be there.

"Well, shit," I mutter, trying to ignore the way my stomach tightens. I'd rather have brain surgery than make a speech in front of a large crowd of people. "Is Rosemary okay?" I ask Nadia.

"Yes, he told Irena she's going to be just fine, but she's going to need some support at home for the next few weeks, so he doesn't want to leave her and travel across the country," Nadia says, and I immediately feel a little better knowing Rosemary isn't deathly ill.

I *really, really* detest public speaking. I chew on the inside of my cheek nervously. "Right, of course. It makes sense that he wouldn't want to be so far away if she's not well," I mutter to myself.

"Please, please, please," Nadia says hopefully. "I know you hate public speaking, but this is such a big deal for Irena. You could recycle that speech you gave in Florida," she says, referring to a presentation I gave at a conference a year ago. Normally I wouldn't reuse a speech, but this one wasn't very technical, and it's unlikely anyone from that conference will be at this event. I also practiced the damn thing so much I still know it by heart.

"Oh, man..." I murmur. Dr. Madsen recommending me as his replacement is a huge honor, and I would never want to disappoint him. Plus, the more I can support him, the better the chances are that I'll get his blessing to take over his lab when the time comes.

I blow out a breath. "Of course I'll do it," I say, my heart rate speeding up at the thought.

"Oh, sweetie, thank you so much." Nadia's relieved look is almost enough to make the whole ordeal worthwhile. "I'll call Irena and tell her to stop freaking out. I'm sure she'll be in touch with you later with details."

The day goes by quickly, and before I know it, I'm getting ready to head home for yet another wild Friday night of pizza and a couple of beers before an early bedtime. As I'm walking to my car, the rain still pouring down, my phone pings with a text from my friend Declan.

Declan: Hey. Drinks tonight?

Declan and I met years ago when we were at college doing our undergrad degrees. He's a sports reporter who moved to Seattle a few years before me. We reconnected when I moved here, and he's become a good friend. We usually meet up for drinks or dinner every couple of weeks or so, but it's been a while since I've seen him.

"Well, crap," I mutter under my breath, tossing my messenger bag into the back seat of my car. I'm feeling a little worn down, but I know if Dec is asking to go for drinks, he's feeling antsy. Since it's the holidays, I understand why. He's newly single, having broken up with his longtime girlfriend a few months ago, and he's still struggling to adjust to being unattached. I hate the thought of him sitting alone all night, fighting the urge to contact his ex, who is *not* a good person. And no one wants to be alone at Christmastime.

Settling into the driver's seat, I stare at my phone for a minute before replying. As much as I'd been looking forward to getting home, it will be good for me to get out. Maybe it will stop my anxiety from spiraling out of control over tomorrow night's speech.

Me: Yeah, I'm in.

We make plans to meet up later, and as I head home, I keep telling myself it will be healthy for me to get out of the house. Maybe if I keep repeating it, I'll start to believe it.

CHAPTER 2
Aleks

"Oh my god, do I need this," I mutter to my friend Josie as the bartender hands me a gin and tonic with extra lime.

"Oh, boo, I'm sorry," she says, flipping her curly red hair over her shoulder and taking a sip from her own drink. "Has it been bad again this week?"

"God, Jo, it's a shitshow. Nothing I do makes the coach happy. He's totally convinced the only reason I got this job was because of my dad. Like, he can barely hide his utter contempt for me."

Josie clucks at me like a mother hen. "Oh, honey," she says, giving my arm a sympathetic squeeze as we slide into a booth in the comfortable little bar down the street from my condo.

I'm an equipment manager for Seattle's American Hockey League team, the Emerald City Eagles. We're the minor-league affiliate, or "farm team," for the city's brand-new NHL team, the Seattle Sasquatch. I've been doing it for a year and a half since our team started playing the year before the Sasquatch, and until recently I've loved every second. Things changed last month when they fired their old coach and replaced him with a guy who is not a fan of mine. He assumes the only reason I have the job is because my dad is a well-known former NHL player. It doesn't matter to him that I'm more than qualified, with a business degree in logistics and project management and a lifetime of living and breathing hockey. But he's been making my life a damn living nightmare ever since he arrived, and it's beginning to wear me down.

"I wish I could help you," Jo says. "Just try to keep your eye on the prize, I guess?"

I nod. "Yeah, just letting me bitch to you about it helps." I give her a forlorn smile. "I'm just starting to worry that he's going to start pushing to get me fired."

I come from a hockey family. My father played in the NHL for twenty seasons, my two older brothers still play in the league, and my older sister has been part of two US Olympic Women's Hockey teams. My mom didn't play pro hockey, slouch that she is, but she was an Olympic figure skater. So that leaves me, the only non-athlete in the family. The truth is I like playing hockey just fine, but playing it isn't what I love. What I really want is to build teams, to be the person who creates something special from a random group of players, coaches, and staff. That's the job of a general manager in the NHL, and that's what I want. My goal is to become one of the youngest NHL GMs ever, and this job is an important step toward that, so even if it's shitty, I need to stick it out until I can find a more senior position.

"I'm so sorry, sweet cakes," Josie says. "It's bullshit, but you'll land on your feet. You're smart and organized and resourceful. Plus, you've been kicking ass at this job for over a year. Things will fall into place, one way or another, when the universe knows you're ready."

I have to hold back my eye roll when she drops that little nugget. I love Josie—we've been friends forever—but she's got a few *woo-woo* tendencies that aren't my jam. She's all about crystals and tarot cards and energy vibrations. It's not my thing, but she didn't have anyone or anything else to comfort her when she was growing up with abusive parents, so if her crystals make her feel good, I'm all in. Truthfully, I'm so desperate for things to get better at work maybe a few crystals scattered around my office or the locker room might not be such a bad idea. I mean, it can't hurt, right?

"Well, I just hope the universe can sense I'm ready for a change now. Because this shit is really pissing me off," I mutter sullenly into my drink.

As much as it pisses me off, it's not the first time people have assumed I'm just riding my dad's coattails, and it won't be the last. The truth is my family name did open doors for me, and it probably always will if I want to stay in the hockey world, but the flip side is that it makes people very eager to see me fail. Someone with a name like mine gets a lot fewer chances to fuck up. I might have been born into this game, but I've also worked really damn hard, and I love it just as much as anyone. I'm willing to pay my dues, but I don't want to be constantly having to prove that I'm capable.

"Okay, stop stewing," Josie says before taking a sip from her drink and checking her phone for texts. "It's

Friday night, and you're off for the weekend. Time to have a little fun."

I heave a sigh, resolving to put work out of my head for the rest of the night. I glance around, surveying the place for anyone of interest. After the week I've had, I deserve a little no-strings-attached fun. It's one of my rare weekends off since the team doesn't play until Monday, but I do have a charity event tomorrow night. I'll be rubbing elbows with pro athletes and sports execs from around the country, so I'll need to be on my best behavior. That means if I want a little weekend action, tonight's the night.

I'm casting my gaze around the room to see if anyone piques my interest when I see him. *Holy shit on a shingle.* I let out an audible gasp, causing Josie to look up at me from across the table.

"What?" she says, but I just shake my head, and she goes back to her phone.

The man is... *wow*... Wavy, dark brown hair falls just over the tops of his ears and across the back of his neck, with just a hint of gray at the temples, making him look distinguished AF. Stylish horn-rimmed glasses frame chocolate-brown eyes above his neatly trimmed beard, and a simple, well-fitted gray T-shirt hugs his muscular chest. Bold ink in a design I can't quite make out covers his left arm, and I would bet my life that under those comfortable-looking khakis, his ass is a goddamn work of art.

Josie looks up from her phone again and promptly cranes her head around to see what's got me staring and probably drooling on the table.

"Stop it!" I hiss, and she turns back to me with a knowing smile.

"Oh, I see how it is." She waggles her eyebrows. "I'm gonna get ditched for that DILF over there, right?"

I sputter at her. "He's not a DILF," I say indignantly.

She grins like a Cheshire cat. "Mmmm-hmmm. Well, he's some kind of ILF, that's for damn sure. But you're lucky. Tara's on her way, so you're free. Go claim your treat, and you don't have to feel guilty for leaving me."

I shoot her a little eye roll, but it's understated because she's one hundred percent correct. The guy is definitely some kind of ILF, and I really do want him to be my treat for the night.

"Go!" She shoos me away and grabs her phone again. "Go get your reward for making it through a long and exhausting week. And call me tomorrow because I need details."

I grab my drink and slide out of the booth, but before walking away, I lean over to smack a big, juicy kiss on her cheek. "Thanks, lovey. I owe you for this one. I definitely need to—ahem—blow off a little steam."

"I know, I know. Go, enjoy. Have fun and be safe," she says.

I give her a grateful smile. "I promise. Love you, Jo."

Giving her one last little wave, I turn around to see if I can nail down this incredible specimen for tonight. *Nail* being the operative word.

CHAPTER 3
Ben

Draining the last of my beer, I survey the bar while I wait for Declan to return with more drinks. I rarely have more than one if I'm going to be behind the wheel, but tonight, I need another. Stupid nerves about tomorrow night's speech. *Fucking hell, how did I let myself get talked into that again?* Public speaking is one of my greatest fears. It's ridiculous. I'm a brain surgeon, for god's sake. In surgery, one tiny slip and I could literally kill someone. That pressure, I can handle with no problem, but the thought of standing up in front of a room of people, everyone's eyes glued to me while I try desperately to sound like I know what I'm talking about, that makes me weak in the knees.

The bar is busy tonight, and even though I'm not big on crowds, it's still comfortable. The staff went above and beyond decorating for the holidays.

Old-fashioned decorations like holly, mistletoe, and pine garlands are everywhere, and a Christmas tree covered in multicolored twinkle lights sits in one corner. More string lights and the flickering votive candles on each table make it feel warm and cozy, especially in contrast to the freezing cold rain outside. Sounds of laughter and conversation blend together with Christmas music to make it seem like we're all in a cozy little bubble. Part of me imagines how much nicer my weekend would be if I could just stay here, all wrapped up in toasty holiday feels.

Releasing a sigh, I glance at my watch, and when I look up, there's a guy approaching our table. Younger than me, probably in his midtwenties, he's clean-shaven with light blond hair that looks just about ready for a cut. He's maybe five foot seven, but what he lacks in physical size, he seems to make up for with the vibe he puts out, which for some reason makes him seem physically bigger. I don't know if it's his confident walk or the smirk on his face that's *just* this side of cocky, but I can't take my eyes off him. He's wearing skinny jeans paired with a light brown cashmere sweater over a collared shirt. Behind his horn-rimmed glasses are unusually bright green eyes, easy to see even though he's still several feet away. He's got the preppy-nerd look down pat, and I am here for it. He glides to a stop in front of me and flashes a brilliant smile.

"Hi there," he says, his gaze friendly and inviting.

"Hi, yourself," I say.

"I'm Aleks."

I take the hand he holds out, noticing how his smaller hand gets swallowed up by my big paw. His palm is cool against mine, and our handshake goes on just a half second longer than normal. "Hi, Aleks. I'm Ben."

He licks his lips, and my dick twitches in my pants. *Jesus, it's been way too long since I got laid.*

"So, Ben, I realize this might be the cheesiest pickup line of all time, but I don't think I've seen you around here before," he says, one side of his mouth curling up in a coy smile.

I chuckle. "I tend to work a lot of hours, so by the time Friday rolls around, I'm usually more interested in crashing on my couch than partying." *Way to make myself sound irresistible.*

"Mmmm," he hums. "I hear that. I'm here recovering after a long week myself tonight." He takes a sip from his drink, looking up at me from beneath his eyelashes. "So, what do you do that leaves you too tired to come out on Fridays?" he asks, his tongue darting out to lick his lips.

"I'm a doctor," I say, and he gives me a skeptical look.

"Really?" he says. "Are you *actually* a doctor, or is that just a line?" His eyes have a teasing glimmer to them.

"It's the unfortunate truth," I say, smiling. "I'm a surgeon and a researcher."

His mouth forms a perfect O, and then he juts out one hip, placing one hand on it, as if he's about to give me a lecture. "*Really*? An *actual* surgeon?"

I bark out a laugh. "An actual surgeon, I promise. It's not the most glamorous job though. If I was feeding you a line, I'd probably say I was something a lot more exciting. Maybe an astronaut. Or some kind of pro athlete. Those both sound sexier than 'doctor'."

He snorts. "The astronaut thing might impress me, but FYI, if you want to pick me up, pretending to be a pro athlete isn't gonna get you very far."

"Oh? Why is that?" I lift an eyebrow.

He rolls his eyes and scrunches up his nose like he smells something unpleasant. "I grew up with athletes. Two older brothers, my sister, and my dad are all big into sports. Athletes do *not* do it for me. I've seen how that particular type of sausage is made."

"I see." I give him an amused smile. "I'm sure there's a joke in there somewhere about sausages, but I'll let it go for now."

Those sparkling green eyes of his must have some kind of magnetic power because I can't seem to pull my own gaze away from them, and the smile he shoots me is full of mirth.

"Can I join you?" Aleks asks, and I wave at one of the empty chairs at our table.

"Make yourself comfortable. My buddy just went to grab us a couple more drinks."

He pulls out the chair next to me and gracefully slides into it, leaning in close. Under the table, his knee brushes against mine, and I'm hyperconscious of where he's touching me.

We're silent for a couple of moments, but it's not uncomfortable. The air between us is charged, but even though I'm usually nervous in these situations, Aleks isn't bringing up those feelings in me. I mean, yes, it's clear we've both got one thing on our minds, but we're not trying to intimidate each other. I don't know why, but something about him makes me feel instantly comfortable.

When Declan reappears, he places my rum and Coke in front of me but doesn't sit back down. "Thanks, man," I say, wrenching my gaze away from Aleks. "Declan, this is Aleks. Aleks, my friend Dec."

"Hey, nice to meet you," Dec says easily, and Aleks gives him a little wave and a smile.

When I look up, my friend is looking at me with a barely suppressed grin. "So, I was just chatting with that girl over at the bar." He inclines his head toward a pretty dark-haired woman. "You cool here?"

I chuckle, not entirely sure whether he was actually talking to the girl or if he sees what's happening between Aleks and me and wants to make himself scarce.

"Yeah, sure," I say, narrowing my eyes at him, trying to see whether he's telling the truth.

He just gives me a cheeky smirk. "I'll catch you in a little bit, okay?" he tosses over his shoulder as he takes off toward the bar, and a second later, I see him talking to the woman.

I turn back toward Aleks.

"Now, *that's* a good friend," he observes playfully, taking another drink.

"Usually, I'm his wingman, not the other way around," I laugh.

It turns out Aleks is easy to talk to. We don't exchange a lot of personal details, but it's almost like we don't need to. I feel like I already know him, which makes no sense, but I'm not about to stop and question it. Not if this night is heading where I think it is.

I'm not normally a hookup guy; I'm more of a serial dater. But I've spent most of my adult life busting my ass in med school and everything that's been part of my career since then. Since most guys I meet aren't usually into dating, my experience is pretty goddamn limited. It's not like I *never* hook up, but I don't usually like the way I feel the next day, so that means my sex life has leaned strongly toward *pathetic* for a very long time.

As the evening passes, I actually manage to relax, and not only am I *not* obsessing about tomorrow night's speech, but I'm genuinely having a good time. Aleks is funny and sweet, and I allow myself to relax and enjoy a few more drinks than usual. If we end up spending the night together, and that's looking promising, I can swing by in the morning for my car. For tonight, I'm not going to worry about anything other than feeling good and making sure he feels good. Maybe giving my brain a time-out and a couple of healthy orgasms will help keep me calm for my speech tomorrow night.

I'm comfortably tipsy, and I think Aleks is, too, as we've gradually maneuvered our chairs closer to each other. I look up to see Declan approaching, holding hands with the dark-haired woman he's been talking with most of the evening.

"Hey," he says, looking a little tipsy himself. "Ben, this is Chloe. Chloe, meet my friend Ben and his friend Aleks."

"Hello," the woman says politely with a friendly smile. Declan beams at her.

Uh-oh, I think. Declan has made some regrettable choices in girlfriends over the past couple of years. His most recent ex was the worst of the bunch, but she certainly wasn't the only one. I think Dec's issue is that he wants to meet that right person so badly he attracts the ones who are in it for the wrong reasons. But this Chloe seems nice enough, and I'm not about to cockblock my friend, especially when I'm on the verge of getting laid myself for the first time in months.

"So, I'm going to make sure Chloe gets home okay," Declan says with a smile. "You all good here?" His gaze moves between Aleks and me.

"We're all good," I say. "You're not driving, right?" I check, noting his slightly slurred words. I know he'd never take a chance on driving after drinking, but taking care of my friends comes so naturally to me I do it without even thinking.

He nods. "Yup. I'll come back and get my car... umm, later. I, uh, just want to make sure she gets home okay, you know..." He gives Chloe another bright smile.

Chloe lets out an unladylike snort and then covers her mouth with her hand, turning red with embarrassment. "Oops, sorry," she giggles. "But that was hilarious. Pretty sure we're all grown-ups here. You can just say we're going home together." She's still smiling, and Declan looks abashed.

I chuckle. Chloe already seems better than his most recent ex. At least she's got a sense of humor. "Go on, have fun, you guys." I grin at them.

They both give us a little wave before turning to head out, and then it's just Aleks and me.

"I don't know about you, but I think they've got the right idea," he says, waggling his eyebrows and making me laugh. He puts his hand on my thigh, sliding it up toward where my desperately hard cock is trapped in my pants. It jumps like it's trying to get closer to him. He bites his bottom lip and looks up at me.

"Can I interest you in a drink at my place?" He gives my inner thigh a suggestive squeeze, and I can barely hold back a groan.

A devious grin crosses his face, and he slides his hand up, cupping my dick and letting his hand rest there. This time, I have to bite the inside of my cheek to stop my obscene moan from escaping.

"That sounds like an excellent idea," I say, my voice sounding breathless to my own ears. In a flash, Aleks stands, extending his hand for me to grab.

"Thank god," he says with a grin as I grab my coat off the back of the chair, and we head for the door.

CHAPTER 4
Ben

We stumble out of the bar as our rideshare pulls up, and on the short ride to his place, Aleks and I can't keep our hands off each other. If the dirty looks the driver gives us are any indication, we probably earn ourselves a very low passenger rating, but I can't find it in me to care. I haven't had sex with anyone but myself in months, and my body is *very* excited about the current situation. I don't remember ever wanting someone as badly as I want this man. I'm not familiar with this desperate feeling, and it's uncomfortable but with an edge of pleasure. It's almost like the discomfort is a signal that I'm alive. Whatever it is about him, I am completely on board.

The Uber pulls up in front of a beautiful building in Capitol Hill. It's stylish and modern, the front façade made up of glass and black metal, while the other sides look like red brick. A wreath made from live pine boughs hangs from the glass main entry door, and white twinkle lights are strung around the entryway, giving the building an elegant but festive feel. Aleks drags me out of the car and quickly unlocks the front door. He punches the elevator call button, but when the doors don't open fast enough for him, he grabs my hand, yanking me toward the staircase.

"Come on," he says roughly. "I can't wait for the fucking elevator." He runs up the first flight of stairs, turning to look at me when he reaches the landing. I'm on him immediately, pushing him up against the wall and attacking his mouth while he gives as good as he gets. Finally, he wrenches his lips off mine, panting heavily. "Goddamn, I'm about to make you fuck me right here in the stairwell, and then I'll get kicked out of my condo. A couple more flights, let's go."

He turns, taking the stairs two at a time, which seems like it would be a challenge since he's not the tallest guy, but he must be in great shape because he's not even winded when we finally reach his floor. A few moments later, he unlocks his apartment and drags me inside, kicking the door shut behind him. It's dark inside, with only a small light from under the cabinets and the streetlights from outside providing any visibility, but it doesn't matter. The only thing I want to see is Aleks underneath me. Or on top of me—at this point, I don't even care; I just want him. Somehow, we make it up one final set of stairs to the sleeping area of his loft, barely taking our mouths off each other. As soon as we're in his bedroom, I'm all over him like the proverbial moth to a flame.

"Fuck, finally," he murmurs as I crash my mouth into his. He curls his fists into the material of my shirt and arches into me, his cock pressing into mine through our clothes. Instinctively, I thrust against him, a groan escaping me as he moves his hands around my waist, sliding them up under my T-shirt, his palms cool against the warm skin of my back.

He pushes us away from the wall, walking us backward toward his bed, where I fall on my back, and he follows me down. Somewhere along the way, we've both ditched our glasses, and his eyes sparkle in the light trickling in from the outside. His pupils are blown out, and we hold each other's gaze for a moment before he lowers his head to place a line of soft kisses along my jawline to my ear, where he takes the lobe into his mouth and bites down hard enough to sting.

I hiss with surprise and then shock him by flipping us over quickly so he's underneath me. I pause, staring down at him. We're both panting, and his cheeks are flushed. He's fucking beautiful.

"You're wearing too many clothes," I murmur, shimmying back to straddle his hips. Grasping the edge of his shirt, I pull upward. "Sit up."

He complies wordlessly with the soft command, eyes never leaving mine. After stripping off our shirts, we crash back together, and a sharp breath catches in my throat at the press of his hot skin against mine. "So fucking good," I whisper into his neck before dragging my tongue slowly along his collarbone, then moving lower again and attaching my mouth to his nipple, biting down. He groans, grabbing the back of my head and sliding his fingers into my hair, pulling hard enough to sting. A hiss escapes me. *Fuck, that feels amazing.*

I move to his other nipple and give it the same treatment as the first while he whimpers and sighs, his hips rocking against me in search of friction. Shuffling backward again, I unbuckle his belt while planting kisses along his belly, reveling in the noises he makes. Knowing he's making those sounds for me sets me on fire. He's so responsive I could almost come just by getting him off. *So. Fucking. Hot.*

"Hips up," I murmur, and he follows my command easily, his eyes fixed on mine as I tug his jeans off. I nuzzle into his groin, mouthing at the soft cotton of his boxer briefs and inhaling his scent as he groans. I'm like some kind of animal, getting off on his smell.

"Jesus, you smell good," I rasp.

He pulls at my shoulders. "Come up here." His voice is hoarse. I move quickly, taking his mouth again and groaning at his incredible taste.

"We both need to be naked for this to work properly." He smiles into my mouth, and I can't help but snort a laugh. Sassy little thing.

"I think you should ask me a little more nicely than that," I murmur back before kissing him again. Fuck, his kisses are like a drug. He arches up and pushes me off, a smirk playing at his kiss-swollen lips as he quickly shucks his underwear, tossing them to the floor.

"Should I? What if I took what I want without asking at all?"

I'm on my knees, straddling his hips, and he grinds his dick up into mine to make his point, a look of pure mischief on his face.

I laugh loudly, which feels strange at first. I've never thought of sex as *funny*. But then I realize that not only am I turned on and having a good time, but I'm genuinely having fun. *What is it with this guy?* He's bringing out stuff in me I never even knew was there. But I'm not about to engage in any serious self-reflection right now since I've got an incredibly hot man underneath me, still wearing a shit-eating grin and not much else.

Aleks reaches up to grab at the button of my pants, then sits up and pushes me back so my head is at the foot of the bed, and he's gazing down at me with a hungry look in his eyes. I lift my hips obligingly while he slides off my offending pants and underwear and tosses them onto the floor. He moves so he's on his hands and knees, arms on either side of my hips and his mouth hovering over my achingly hard cock. Our gazes lock as he lowers his head and carefully licks one long, continuous stripe up my underside from my balls to my slit, where he takes a moment to dip his tongue, tasting the precome gathered there. I can't wrench my eyes away as he moans like I'm the best thing he's ever tasted.

"Mmmm," he whispers, "I'm gonna need more of *that*."

He wraps his lips around my crown and sucks, hard. Fire rips through me from my dick to my balls, and I arch into him, gasping as all my muscles tense. "Oh, my god." I whimper and gasp as he works me over, the suction exquisite. I squeeze my eyes shut, trying desperately not to explode because I never, ever want this to end. The moments stretch on until I'm writhing and babbling underneath his ministrations. When I start to lose my grip on control, certain I'm about to come, I push on his shoulders, warring with my own body as I try to resist chasing his mouth with my dick as he pulls off me. "I'm too close," I gasp.

"Oh fuck," he moans, and an instant later, his mouth is on mine again. My own precome is salty on his tongue, and I shudder at how hot it is to taste myself on him.

"Will you fuck me?" he gasps into my mouth, and I groan.

"Jesus Christ, yes."

"Thank god. I'm dying for it."

"Fuuuck," I curse, and I have to reach down to grab my own cock, encircling the base and trying to hold back the orgasm desperately trying to break loose.

I exhale shakily. "I need inside you *right fucking now*."

"Mmm, glad we're in agreement," he says, moving so his face is directly over mine again. He chuckles and moves in to kiss me, but instead, he shifts quickly, grabbing something from his nightstand. Before I can protest, he tosses two condoms and a bottle of lube onto the bed beside us, smiling triumphantly before settling back atop me, our bodies completely intertwined. I run my hands over his compact but strong shoulders, down his back, over his narrow waist to his perfect, round ass, caressing him gently at first before pulling his cheeks apart roughly, enjoying his gasp of surprise. He scrambles for the lube, quickly slicking up his fingers, and I hold him open while he reaches behind himself to prep. A moment later, he closes his eyes and groans as I feel him slide a finger inside himself. My cock jumps in response. Jesus, he is utterly breathtaking. His face is flushed, the color extending all the way down his neck and over his collarbones. When he lets out another groan, my dick twitches yet again, and I'm afraid I'm going to come before I can get inside him.

"Let me," I whisper roughly, snagging the lube and dumping a healthy amount into my hand. I reach around and smear it all over his crack, taking care to make sure my fingers are nice and slick before I slowly slide one into his body beside the two of his own already in there. He lets out another groan as we work together to stretch him.

"Fuck yes, oh fuck yes, fuck. One more. Give me one more, then I'll be ready for your cock," he pants raggedly.

"Happily," I murmur, sliding another finger inside him. Before long, he's actively fucking back against our hands, so I use my other arm around his back, anchoring him close to me, preventing him from moving. He lets out a whine.

"You ready?" I whisper harshly.

Aleks nods sharply before croaking out, "Can I ride you?"

"Fuck! Fuck, yes, please. God, get on me."

"Condom," he gasps.

"Shit! Sorry, almost forgot." I snatch the package off the bed, tearing it open and suiting up as fast as humanly possible, then take another healthy handful of lube and slick myself up. I hold my dick at the base, pointing straight up as Aleks gets back into position, his ass directly above my straining cock.

Time seems to stop as he slowly, slowly, lowers himself onto me. My cock slides past his first tight ring of muscle, and he pauses a moment, adjusting to the stretch. From my position under him, he's stunning, a rosy flush spreading from his cheeks down his neck and over his chest. His head is thrown back, and a strangled noise escapes him as he slides down another inch or so, and holy hell, I've never, ever felt anything this good. I have to bite the inside of my cheek so hard the metallic taste of blood fills my mouth, but it works, buying me a little more time so I don't come like a goddamn rocket before Aleks. Because there's no way I'm going to let myself come before he does.

Aleks

Holy mother of fuck. This cock inside me, this man underneath me... This is way more than just a random fuck. As my body slowly opens to let him in, something settles inside me. I can't describe it, but it just feels *right*. I know that sounds like something out of a romance novel, but it's honestly weird. His dick, his body, even the sound of his voice, it all feels like it was built specifically for me. It's fucking incredible. I've had a fair amount of sex in my life, but this feels like I just leveled up. I need to go slowly, otherwise I'm going to go off like a shot, and this will be over far too soon.

"Fuck, yes. Ride me. Oh god, just like that. Ohhh." Ben is almost incoherent as I rock back and forth over him until he's fully seated inside me. I look down and lose my breath at the sight of this stunning, perfectly put-together man coming undone underneath me. I roll my hips against his so he slides over my prostate, and we groan together. A drop of sweat slides down his temple, and I lean down to lick it, gasping as the change in position somehow, impossibly, feels even better. We're both breathing heavily, and when I move so I can see his face, our eyes lock, something passing between us. I don't know what it is, but my chest squeezes, and Ben's eyes widen slightly, like he feels something too. A moment later, he thrusts up into me roughly, and it's ecstasy. We find our perfect rhythm right away, moving together like we've rehearsed this. Our faces are only inches apart, mouths open, breaths mingling, our gazes still locked together. He grabs the back of my head, pulling me down into a blistering kiss, thrusting his tongue into my mouth as he thrusts up into my body, and I collapse against him. And that's it. Our instincts take over, our bodies writhing together, his cock sliding in and out of my hole. The scent of us, sweat and musk and lust, hangs in the air as we keep moving, not so much kissing as breathing into each other as we lurch forward, chasing our release.

I push on his chest, leaning back so my weight is on my knees, so I can fuck into him as hard as he's fucking me, our bodies slamming together with delicious, filthy sounds.

"Oh, god, oh yes, oh yes," I chant as his hard cock slams against my prostate over and over again, causing sparks to burst behind my tightly closed eyelids.

His rhythm stutters, and he grabs my hips so tightly I'm certain I'll have bruises as our bodies keep slamming together. Then he stills, the corded muscles in his neck pulled tight, the smallest whimper escaping him as his cock pulses and throbs inside me as he comes and comes. That whimper is what pulls me over. I let out a roar as my orgasm rolls through me in powerful waves. I cover his abdomen in my release, shooting almost painfully until I collapse, my body limp against his, my come sticky between our bodies, utterly spent as we lie together, both gasping for air.

CHAPTER 5
Ben

It's pitch-dark when I wake up a few hours later, my mouth as dry as if I've been chewing on cotton balls. Aleks' warm body is curled into mine, and it's surprisingly comfortable. His bed is soft and cozy, but my head is pounding, and I need to piss like a racehorse, so I slide carefully out from under the sheet and pad quietly into the bathroom. After relieving myself and grabbing a couple of Tylenol from a bottle on the shelf, I realize this hangover is going to require more than just a swallow of water from the bathroom faucet. After snagging my boxers off the floor, I tiptoe quietly down the stairs to the sleek, modern kitchen below. This loft is something else. Whatever his job is, Aleks must be doing pretty damn well to afford a place like this. I'm not even sure my doctor's salary would be enough to afford this gorgeous loft.

I drink my first glass of ice water down in one long swallow, immediately going back for a second. By the time I get to glass number three, I'm no longer parched, but I know if I can force down a bit more, it will do wonders for what feels like it could turn into a serious hangover.

I sigh. Not exactly a smart move. It's unlike me to go out and get wasted, especially with an important event the next day, but I can't find it in myself to regret it because if I hadn't loosened up enough to come home with Aleks, I would have missed out. And that, whatever that was with him, was unlike any other experience I've had. Taking a step back from the fridge, I wander over to the redbrick feature wall. He's got a few shelves mounted on it featuring framed photos and other mementos. His space is warm and comfortable but masculine. I like it.

I wander slowly around the perimeter of the living room, running my hand along the soft faux-fur throw draped over the back of the couch. As I get to the bookshelves on either side of his modern glass fireplace, I take a closer look at the pictures. Several of them feature Aleks with what must be his siblings, three smiling kids with their arms around each other's shoulders and one child who looks quite a bit younger. I smile. Aleks is definitely the baby of his family. The photos feature them at various ages over the years, and even once they get to adulthood, his sister and brothers tower over him. The brothers look familiar to me for some reason, but all the recent photos appear to be taken on beach vacations, as they're always wearing sunglasses. I grin, thinking of my own sister, Lauren, an ER doctor at a hospital on Seattle's Eastside. I should really take the time to add some family pictures to my own living room; it makes the place feel more like a home. I carefully replace a photo of the siblings on some kind of yacht in beautiful, turquoise water and amble back to the shelves on the feature wall, curious to learn more about the man who literally rocked my world a few hours ago.

I'm almost finished my third glass of water when I notice a photo of what must be his entire family, or at least that's what I assume. I huff out a laugh, realizing that the family is posing with a life-size replica of the Stanley Cup. My stepdad played professional hockey for years, and obviously, my research into head injuries keeps me close to the hockey community, so I pick it up to take a closer look. I smile since it's still kind of rare to find American families who are into hockey the way so many Canadians are. They're goofing around in the photo. The cup is on the floor right in front of the man who must be Aleks' dad. He's poised with a big spoon right over it like he's about to dig into a giant ice-cream sundae. Aleks' mom sits beside him, squeezing a big bottle of chocolate syrup into the bowl of the iconic trophy. The three older kids are sitting on the couch making faces while a little kid, who I assume is a four- or five-year-old Aleks, is on the floor at his dad's feet with his little arms wrapped around the base of the big trophy while pressing a kiss to it. I start to chuckle until I take another look at the cup itself, realizing it's not a replica—the family is posing with the real thing. My heart racing, I step over to the window to get a better look under the light from the streetlight outside. I do a double take, and the bottom drops out of my stomach.

My stepdad, Bob, played in the NHL for a long time, but his career was cut short when he took a vicious hit that knocked him out cold and gave him a concussion so serious that no doctor would sign off on his return to the ice. The league ruled the hit legal, but most people agreed it was right on the line and could have—maybe *should* have—been a major penalty. And the player who delivered that life-changing hit to Bob? None other than Kent Warren, the man in Aleks' family photo.

Oh my god, I need to get out of here. Aleks' father is Kent Warren.

CHAPTER 6
Aleks

B linking my eyes open, I take a quick survey of my bedroom. After noting that everything looks like it's supposed to look and wondering briefly why the hell I'm awake so early, I close my eyes again and try to go back to sleep. Until approximately 2.1 seconds later when the events of last night come flooding back to me. The bar, the fun conversation and flirting with Ben, bringing him back to my loft, and then the next few hours of utter sexual satisfaction and complete bliss.

I think last night qualifies as one of the top three sexual experiences of my life. *Okay, fine. Who am I kidding?* That was, without a doubt, the hottest, most amazing night of sex I've ever had, hands down. The way he played my body was like some kind of master violinist, which is a ridiculously cheesy thing to say, but it fits. Ben seemed to know exactly what to do to make me feel *un-fucking-believable.* It was like he could read my mind and my body, knowing what I wanted even before I did. And if my ability to read body language is worth anything, I'm pretty sure he was just as blown away by our connection as me.

Hoping he'll be up for a repeat this morning, I reach over to find him, only the sheets next to me are cold; my spacious king-sized bed is empty.

"Well, crap," I murmur, my fantasies of mutual wake-up blowjobs evaporating. Instead, I indulge in a luxurious stretch and a big yawn before rolling out of bed and into the bathroom. After taking care of business, Ben still hasn't returned, so I snag a pair of gray sweats off the edge of my big, rarely used bathtub and head down to the kitchen.

By the time I've reached the bottom of the stairs, it's obvious he's not here. *Huh.* Maybe he's an early riser and popped out to grab us coffee and breakfast. He probably left a note. Padding into my kitchen, I glance around to find the counters just as clear as they were last night. The only sign that someone has even been in here is an empty glass sitting beside the sink. That's it. No note. My phone is sitting on the coffee table, so I grab it. He probably texted. *Shit... We never exchanged numbers.* The phone in my hand stays rudely silent while I stare down at it blankly as if it's going to provide me with answers. Running a hand through my messy hair, I survey my loft again, looking for some kind of explanation, but I come up empty.

"Maybe he decided to go to the really good breakfast place. The line's always crazy there," I mutter to myself. But deep down, I know that's just my optimistic side clinging to the last scraps of hope. I've been ghosted; it couldn't be more obvious.

"Whatever," I mumble. Setting my phone down, I head to the kitchen for coffee. Strangely, I'm not hungover. I guess the hours we spent riding the old bony express must have burned off all the alcohol in my system.

Waiting for my coffee to be ready, I replay the night in my head, but I can't find a good reason for him to have bolted. I mean, it's not like it's so unusual. I've certainly left a hookup in the middle of the night before, and people have left me too. It's never bothered me one bit. So, the question is, why am I even sparing a second thought for this Ben guy? I mean, yeah, he's hot, and yeah, we were *fire* in bed. But we're strangers. We don't owe each other anything. *Why the hell am I even concerned?*

I shake my head like I'm literally trying to ditch these unsettling feelings as I add a liberal amount of cream and sugar to my coffee. But I can't stop thinking about him. The way Ben's touch sent shivers down my spine right from the first moment our fingers brushed against each other at the bar. The way his kiss felt almost worshipful, like he couldn't get enough of me. The way our bodies pressed together, desperate to make sure there wasn't one millimeter of space between us. A delicious shiver rolls through me as I stand at my kitchen counter, remembering how he felt inside me, like his body was made to fit with mine. How hot it was that he never broke eye contact, watching me intently while I came, and then how he looked when he finally let himself go, surrendering to his own release.

Jesus fuck. Yeah. No doubt about it. It was the best sex I've ever had, and the fact that he took off can only mean one thing: he didn't feel the same way. The connection I felt was all in my head.

"Well, fuck that," I grumble aloud—again. Apparently, incredible sex turns me into a weirdo who walks around alone in his house making conversation with himself. Maybe I need to get a cat. At least that way, I can tell myself that's who I'm talking to.

I walk over to my window and stare outside. It's another cloudy, drippy day in Seattle. I mean, it's the time of year when nothing else should be expected, but for some reason, it pisses me off this morning. I wonder what Ben's doing today? I wonder if I'd run into him if I went back to the pub.

"*Fuck. That*," I snarl. I refuse to turn into some sad little puppy, chasing some guy around, no matter how amazing the sex is. *I. Will. Not. Be. That. Guy.* Been there and done that.

I head back upstairs to change into running clothes. Yeah, going for a run is about the last thing I feel like doing, but maybe a little pain will take my mind off things. Plus, I'll feel better for tonight's big gala with the Sasquatch team. Several players and members of management are coming to this fundraiser for brain injury research, including the team's GM, Carson Wells. People from all over the pro sports world will be there, so tonight is a chance for me to make some useful connections. I'm gunning for an NHL-level job. I know I haven't been working for the farm team all that long, but I've always known the NHL is where I want to be.

I've been hearing rumors that Wells has been trying to persuade the ownership group to participate in some kind of new project around player safety. It has something to do with a new type of helmet designed to reduce head injuries. I only know about it because the Sasquatch's equipment manager, who is indirectly my boss, told me about it on the down-low because they may need some extra staff to help the Sasquatch technicians care for the new equipment. It's all confidential, but if it gets the go-ahead, I might have a chance to work some NHL games with their technicians. That would get me in front of the players, coaching staff, and maybe even their management team. I sometimes feel like it's taking forever to get into the job I really want, helping to manage a team, but I know these things take time. Gotta walk before I run, I suppose.

Whatever the case, I refuse to fuck up my future by acting like some kind of sad sack simply because I got ditched by a hookup. This guy needs to be relegated to the back of my mind with all my other hookups. Just a pleasant memory. Tonight, my head needs to be fully in the game.

CHAPTER 7
Ben

I wake up bright and early on Saturday morning, assuming it still counts as waking up if you haven't been to sleep. When I got home from Aleks' place, after getting my Uber to drop me at the bar so I could pick up my car, there was no way in hell I could sleep.

What are the chances that the first time I hook up in ages ends up being with an enemy of my family? *Okay, that might be a little dramatic.* But my stepdad lying on the ice, knocked out cold, and then never being able to return to the game was also pretty dramatic, and somehow, I end up in bed with the son of the guy responsible? *Fuck. My. Life, already. Seriously.*

Kent Warren is still active in the NHL as some kind of advisor or something, but our paths have never crossed. I didn't realize he had another kid besides the older ones who are currently NHL players. Not that it would have mattered if I'd known. It's not like it was at the top of my mind.

I ran out of Aleks' place like my ass was on fire, which was a really shitty thing to do. Especially since last night was one of the most intense experiences of my life. The depth and rawness of our connection... I don't even have words for it. Guilt over the way I took off on him is eating at me because I'm more respectful than that. He didn't deserve to be ditched without a word, but in the moment, all I could think about was getting away. *Fuck.*

I'm showered and ready to go before 9:00 a.m. Problem is, I don't have anywhere to go. I usually visit my stepdad on Sundays, not Saturdays. But after an hour or so of pacing around my condo like a trapped animal, I decide I'll just head over there early.

It's still drizzling when I arrive at the specialized care home. A few years back, it became apparent that Bob was going to need more care than my mom could provide on her own, so they decided to move to Seattle since, by some strange quirk of fate, my sister and I both ended up living here. They found an incredible, supportive home for Bob in Bellevue, just on the east side of Lake Washington, and they bought a lovely condo with a water view only a few blocks away. They both lived in the condo for a couple of years before Bob decided he wanted to move into the memory care facility. His balance had become a lot worse, and though it was a difficult decision, his memory lapses were becoming dangerous, to the point where even he knew it. The frustration experienced by patients with dementia can often result in them lashing out, sometimes even becoming violent. For someone like Bob, with his size and extensive experience with fighting, having him live alone with my mom wasn't a good idea.

My mom's BMW is parked in one of the visitor spots when I get there. I guess she drove today because of the rain. Even though this place is lovely, my stomach is always a mess of knots when I first arrive. The problem is we never quite know what version of Bob we'll get when we visit. It's one of the many shit things about dementia; it literally changes your personality. The kindest, sweetest person can end up being viciously mean, and it's heartbreaking for everyone involved.

The facility itself is beautiful, and the staff does everything possible to keep it from feeling like a hospital. At least the years my stepdad spent getting his ass kicked for the entertainment of hockey fans paid him well. Because he can afford it, he has access to the best care in the best setting possible. But all the little niceties mean shit to my mom, who, for the second time in her life, had her partner ripped away from her by fate. My biological father, JJ, was killed in a car accident when I was a baby. She and Bob Prescott met and married when I was pretty young, so I've never known anyone else as my dad. But because of his brain injury, my mom once again gets fucked out of all the dreams they shared of things they wanted to do once he retired from the game. They're barely even in their sixties— they should be traveling and enjoying the money, not using it to pay for high-end medical care. My mom is amazing though, and somehow, she manages to stay positive and optimistic through everything. Honestly, she's one of my heroes. I don't know how she does it.

I take a breath as I turn the corner to where Dad's suite is located. The door is propped open, which probably means there's a nurse or a care aide in with him, so I knock softly and peek my head around the door. My mom is sitting in the living room of the apartment-style suite. It really is beautiful, and the things that make it suitable for someone who has trouble with mobility and balance are barely notice-able. The windows look out onto a dog park, and on sunny days, he likes to watch the dogs playing and living their best lives.

"Ben, sweetie, what are you doing here today?" my mom asks when she sees me. She hops up from her chair and comes over to give me a squeeze. "Corinna is just helping Bobby with his shower. They'll probably be out in a few minutes," she says. "Can I get you anything? Is it too late for coffee? There's other stuff in the fridge as well. Just grab whatever you feel like."

I return her hug, leaning in to place a kiss on her cheek. "Thanks, Mom. I'll grab a coffee." I hang my coat in the alcove and head into the small kitchen, where there's a Keurig and a big basket of K-Cups on the counter.

After doctoring it up with plenty of cream and sugar, I make my way back to the living room where the care aide, Corinna, is helping my stepdad into his favorite chair.

As usual, my heart twists when I see him. He looks so much older than he is. It's so hard not to clench my fists and rage out loud at the universe sometimes.

"Ben, you're here early!" Dad says once he's comfy in his chair. He gives me a big smile, and some of the tension bleeds out of me as I return it. *Okay. At least we're starting off in a good place for today's visit.* Corinna gives us a wave as she heads out, closing the apartment door behind her.

"Hey, Dad," I say, sitting down in one of the other chairs.

"Trouble sleeping last night, hon?" Mom asks, taking a sip from her coffee. "You've got bags under your eyes."

"No, not... well, actually, yeah, I guess you could say that," I say, staring out the window.

"Anything you want to talk about?" she asks.

I hesitate. I don't know how much to share. I know sometimes talking about his old hockey career can set Dad off, but just as often, bringing up those glory days will push him from a crappy mood into a better place. He seems to be doing well today, so I chance it, catching them up on the speech I'll be making later tonight. When Mom hears that Dr. Madsen's wife isn't well, she gets concerned. When I was going to school in Boston, my parents would visit, and Dr. Madsen is a huge hockey fan. I introduced them, and the four became good friends. Before Bob's condition got too severe, the four of them even took a couple of vacations together. Dennis has been pretty closely involved with my dad's care right from the start, consulting fairly regularly with Dad's doctors here.

"Oh, dear, I hope Rosemary is alright. I'll have to call them this week to check in," she says.

"I think she's okay. At least that's what he told the event organizers. Just sounds like he didn't want to leave her alone at the moment," I say, and my mom nods.

"I know you hate public speaking, honey, but you'll do a great job tonight," she says with an encouraging smile.

"Yeah. Thanks, Mom." I swear, I don't know how the woman stays so positive.

Bob has gone unnaturally quiet, and it's hard to tell what's going on in his head. But the answer becomes clear a minute later when he looks at me with a snarl on his face.

"The *fuck*?" he roars. Instinctively, I move to put myself between my mom and him, but it's doubtful he'll be able to get out of his chair, which, while painful to watch, is a relief. These episodes were a lot scarier when he could move around more easily.

"You're going to help those motherfuckers? You think you're better than me?" he growls, leveling me with a vicious glare. I swallow hard.

"No, Dad, I didn't mean anything. I was just talking about my work, that's all. It doesn't mean anything for you," I say calmly.

Behind me, I feel my mom get up from her chair gingerly. Slowly, she approaches my dad's armchair.

"Bobby, it's okay. You're fine. We're just talking right now," she says in her gentle, reassuring voice, which contains a slight tremor.

Dad doesn't seem to hear her as his eyes become wilder and he starts to shout.

"You think you're better than me? I'll show you who's the real man here! No one does this to me! Nobody!" he yells, his voice rising with each word. His hands clench into fists, and he looks ready to go on a rampage. Without thinking, I grab Mom's arm, yanking her out of his reach. My heart races as rage contorts my dad's face. Suddenly, without warning, he lashes out and slaps me—not hard enough to really hurt, but enough to sting.

I grab my cheek and step back from his chair, swallowing the tears that threaten to spill over. This is so painful. Never in my entire life has he *ever* raised a hand to me. This goddamn disease is eating his brain, and it's devastating to watch.

My mom walks quickly over to the table where her emergency call button is sitting, but I stop her before she can press it. She's supposed to always have it within arm's reach in case anything happens to set him off, but he's been doing so well lately her guard is down.

"Mom, wait, it's okay. Just go get someone. Don't do the whole emergency thing. We're okay." We've only had to use the emergency button a couple of times, and each time, it caused so much stress and chaos that Dad was a mess for days afterward.

She gives me a look and then darts her gaze to my dad, but he seems to have quieted down and is sitting back in his armchair with a dazed look on his face, like he knows something just happened, but he doesn't know what.

My mom hurries to the suite's door, returning moments later with Victor, one of my dad's favorite care aides.

"Bobby, Victor's here to talk with you," she says, her voice a little steadier now.

"Hi, Bob." Victor approaches him slowly, a sunny smile on his face. His unpredictable behavior is one of the biggest reasons Dad insisted on moving into this place, even though it broke both their hearts to do it.

After Victor talks quietly with him for a few minutes, Dad decides he wants to go to bed. He hugs Mom and me like nothing has happened in the last half hour. I guess for him, it hasn't. Sometimes it feels like this disease is a monster that sits around in the corner, patiently waiting to come out as soon as Dad lets his guard down. And once it's come out and caused as much chaos and heartbreak as it can, it disappears back into the corner, sitting patiently until the next opportunity.

The rain has stopped as Mom and I exit the front doors of the residence. As we make our way to our cars, skirting around the puddles in the parking lot, she grabs my arm and gives it a squeeze.

"You okay?" she asks, and I nod, not trusting my voice.

I'm not really okay, but I should be used to this. It's far from the first time it's happened. Finally, I swallow the lump in my throat enough to choke out, "Yeah, I'm okay. Are you?"

She nods as well. The strain on her face is obvious, but there's something else there. She looks defeated, and that is *not* like her. I wrap her in a hug, and she holds on to me tightly for a few minutes.

"It's so hard, Mom. I'm sorry," I whisper, and with one final squeeze, she lets me go, swiping away the tears on her cheeks as she steps back.

"It's okay, hon. It's just hard to watch. You know."

I nod again, blowing out a breath. "Yeah, I do know."

"We got some good news yesterday though," she says. "He was accepted into that drug study we've been hoping for. He's going to be starting the new medication right away."

My eyes widen. "Wow, Mom! Really? That's fantastic news!" I exclaim. One of the leading researchers in the field, who also happens to be an associate of Dr. Madsen's, is running a clinical drug trial on patients with suspected CTE. The rumors are it can work like a miracle, cutting way back on violent outbursts, helping enormously with memory problems and even some of the physical symptoms like balance issues. I didn't think my dad was going to be accepted into the trial since at this stage, they're only taking a tiny number of patients, but I have a sneaking suspicion that my old friend Dr. Madsen may have something to do with him getting chosen. "The early trials were super promising. This is really good news," I tell her.

She smiles, a tiny ray of hope flickering in her eyes. "I hope it slows things down, even a little bit," she says wistfully.

"I hope so too." I give her a hopeful smile. There's really not much anyone can say.

She clears her throat and turns to open her car door before standing on her tiptoes to place a kiss on my cheek. "I'm going to head home. But will you call me tomorrow to let me know how your speech goes tonight?"

When I nod, she gives me another encouraging smile, the same one I remember so well from when I was a kid. Whenever I struggled with anything, my mom's faith in me never ever wavered. "You're going to do an amazing job tonight, Ben, I know it. You feel so passionately about the topic, and you're so knowledgeable. People respond to that kind of sincerity."

"Thanks, Mom. I hope so. I'll call you tomorrow."

We say our goodbyes, and I get into my SUV, heading toward home. My mind is a jumble of nerves about tonight's speech, worry about my parents, and thoughts of Aleks Warren. I can't stop replaying scenes from last night. No matter how much I try to distract myself, I can't help remembering how he looked, the sounds he made, how we felt together... All of it was so fucking hot. Not that it matters. I'll probably never see him again.

It's probably for the best. I could never bring someone from the Warren family into my parents' lives. Not after what Kent Warren did. I think the thing that hurt both my parents the most was that even though the hit was technically legal, the amount of damage it caused was no secret. And Kent never bothered to call Bob to apologize. Not immediately after it happened, and not even when the news broke that my dad would never be able to play again. He and Kent had known each other for years; they'd even been teammates at one point. It was painful for my parents to realize that someone they had respected, even liked, didn't even bother with the courtesy of a phone call to see how he was doing. When the media would ask Kent about it, he would brush off the question or find a way to deflect it. From what I know, he and my dad never spoke again after that hit.

It's that attitude that makes me suspicious of anyone associated with the man or his family; they just don't seem to share the same values as mine. So, no matter how amazing that night was with Aleks, it needs to stay firmly in the past.

It's only been a few hours; that's probably why I can't get him out of my head. Eventually, the memory will fade, and I'll move forward. I have no choice.

CHAPTER 8
Aleks

Stepping out of the shower, I wipe the fog off the mirror and take a long, hard look at myself. There is absolutely no reason I should have spent most of the day moping and feeling sorry for myself simply because a random hookup took off in the middle of the night. Shit, usually, it's a relief when that happens. I've done it myself—sometimes it's just easier to avoid the awkward morning-after chat while trying to figure out the nicest possible way to get the hell out of there. So why the *actual fuck* can I not get Ben out of my mind? What the hell makes him so different? I mean, sure, he's unbelievably good-looking. If I could select a man to represent my "type," he'd look exactly like Ben. And yeah, the way our bodies fit together like puzzle pieces was unlike anything I've felt in my life. But obviously, he didn't feel the same way, and the connection I thought I felt was all in my head. Now

I need to shake it off and get back to business. I did exactly what I'd planned—I blew off some steam and had a little fun. Now I need to get my head screwed on properly because tonight is important for the future of my career.

I slip into my tuxedo quickly. Growing up as part of a big pack of highly decorated athletes, I've been to any number of awards dinners over the years, so I'm used to wearing the penguin suit, but the goddamn bow tie drives me insane. I can never get the damn thing to look right. After a few tries, I finally get it so it's not completely cockeyed, figuring I'll have to ask one of the guys to help me fix it once I get there.

An hour later, I'm walking into the swanky hotel ballroom where the benefit is being held. Round dining tables are draped in white linen, each one adorned with flickering candles of various sizes. Each table's centerpiece is a tall treelike floral sculpture covered in tiny white fairy lights, and subtle blue lighting bathes the room in a soft glow. Overhead, crystal chandeliers glimmer like diamonds in the candlelight. On one side of the room sits an enormous Christmas tree, trimmed in blue and silver and sparkling with the same fairy lights from the centerpieces. I feel like I've stepped into some kind of dream world, and from the murmurs of other guests around me, I'm not the only one who's impressed.

Making my way to one of the bars distributed around the room's edges, I order myself a glass of champagne, simply because the décor seems to invite a fancy drink, and then turn around to survey the room, hoping to find someone I know.

I spot a group of guys standing not far from me, and I immediately recognize them as being from the Sasquatch. Because of the close relationship between the Sasquatch and their farm team, there have been several group functions, so I've been able to get to know several of the players, and one of my favorites is their captain, Rylan Collings. He's played in the league for a while, so I'd met him a few times in the past through my brothers, and he's always struck me as a stand-up guy. He's quiet, but solid, and both Brad and Mike have only nice things to say about him, which is saying something, since my brothers aren't easy to impress. He's standing in a group with a few other players, and Carson Wells is with them. Taking a deep breath, I swallow my nerves and walk over to join them. Making a good impression on our parent-team's GM is important since the better he knows me, the more likely that my name will pop into his head if there are any management opportunities that open up.

"Hey, everyone," I say, approaching their circle.

"Hey, Aleks, how are you?" Austin Cote, another player who's been around the league a while, says with a smile, extending his hand.

I shake his hand, greeting everyone with the most confident smile I can muster. We make small talk for a bit until the three Sasquatch players end up in a friendly debate with a group from another team over some play from an East Coast game last night.

Carson Wells takes a sip from his drink and turns to me.

"So how are you, Aleks?" he asks.

My heart speeds up as my nerves kick in. It's not like me to be anxious around people, but something about Wells intimidates me. He's quiet and stoic, and he doesn't seem to be part of the old boys' club that runs the NHL. He was tapped by Sasquatch ownership to head up the team almost as soon as they were awarded the franchise a few years ago, so he's been part of building the team from the ground up. Even though he's very young for the job and didn't have a ton of NHL experience, he's been incredibly success-ful. It's unheard of for any team to perform so well to-gether in their inaugural season. Carson's been cred-ited with a lot of their success, and it's at least in part due to the huge effort he's put into creating a unique team culture. Everyone attached to the Sasquatch in any way, no matter how minor, is respected and sup-ported, and that attitude starts with Carson himself. Before the start of the season, it wasn't unusual for us to see him around at the Eagles offices to meet with our management or coaches. Some people grumbled about being micromanaged at first, but he proved that he's genuinely interested in finding out what every part of the organization needs in order to be suc-cessful. I'd love to be able to learn the business from someone like him.

"I'm great, thanks, Carson," I say with a smile.

"I'm glad you're here. I was hoping to get a chance to speak to you tonight."

My eyebrows rise. "Oh? What can I help you with?"

He grins. "Actually, it's what I'm hoping you can help me with," he chuckles.

My stomach clenches, wondering what the hell he wants to talk to me about. I hope I haven't fucked up somehow. I know the Eagles coach doesn't like me much, but I'm really hoping he hasn't tried to smear my reputation with the parent team.

"I understand you've been doing a great job with the Eagles. How have you been enjoying it so far?"

I swallow, still confused at what this is about. "I'm really enjoying it. It's been such a great opportunity, and I've been learning so much. We have a great team there."

Carson nods. "Yeah, we do. I'm happy with how things are going. But I also suspect the equipment department isn't where your future ambitions lie, and I wanted to talk to you about an opportunity."

I swallow hard. "Um. Okay, sure." I have no idea what he's talking about, but it doesn't sound like I'm about to get canned, so I've got that going for me.

"We just got approval for a special project, starting in the next couple of weeks," he starts. "I don't know if you're aware, but Dr. Benjamin Jacobs, who's making the keynote speech tonight, has come up with a revolutionary new helmet design. If it works, it could make a big difference in the number of head injuries to hockey players—actually, to all players of contact sports."

Carson pauses and glances around quickly. When he continues, his voice is hushed. "Now, this part won't be officially announced until next week, so please keep it to yourself for now, but he needs to trial the helmets in real-live games at the professional level, and the Sasquatch are going to be part of that trial. Our players are going to be wearing them for a few weeks for the games around the Christmas break so he can gather data."

"Oh, wow, that's amazing," I say. "How will it work?" My mind races with all kinds of questions. It's unusual for any team to make a change to its equipment in the middle of a season. But I like the fact that Wells is positioning the team to be a leader in player safety in a way I haven't seen any other pro-level organization do. It shows they're serious when they talk about wanting the best for their players; they're not only concerned with the almighty dollar.

He nods. "Like I said, we haven't made the official public announcement yet, but we've talked at length with the key players and coaching staff, as well as the Players' Union. It was a... challenge... to get everyone on board, but everyone has been reassured the new helmets shouldn't make any significant difference to what the players feel and see since they're almost exactly the same shape and weight, et cetera, as the ones used now."

"Wow, that's incredible," I say.

"So," he continues. "All of that is a long-winded way of asking if you'd be interested in helping us out with managing the project."

Carter's eyes bore into mine, and my jaw drops open in surprise. I must be misunderstanding because it sounds like he just offered me a position working directly with the Sasquatch. But that can't be right—he must be asking me to support them from my position on the Eagles.

Before I can say anything, he continues. "I'm not entirely sure yet what the job is going to look like, and that's going to be part of the challenge. But basically, you'll be responsible for making sure our equipment techs know how to properly care for everything, and after each game, it will be up to you to make sure all the data gets collected and sent to Dr. Jacobs' team. So, it will mean traveling with the team for away games during that period around the holidays, which I know might be hard since it's a busy time of year. But it will be a great way to showcase your skills as a project manager. It will also get your name in front of the right people. It could ultimately help you achieve some of your career goals."

"Um. Wow. That sounds incredible. Are you thinking this would be a temp position, then?"

Carson's smile grows bigger. "Well, yes, at first, it will be a temp position. But if things go well, I'm fairly certain I can find a permanent place for you in the organization. I'm not sure where that will be, but we're always on the lookout for people with the right combination of personality and skills. I understand you haven't had the easiest time with some of the coaching staff on the Eagles, and I'm sorry about that. But I hear you've handled yourself with incredible professionalism. I know that can be a difficult position to be in, and you've done very well."

"Holy shit," I breathe out and am immediately embarrassed. "Sorry," I mutter. Carson is probably one of the only people I've ever come across in the hockey world who doesn't have the mouth of a drunken sailor. He chuckles.

"Does that mean you're interested?" he asks.

"Fuck yes I am," I say with conviction, and heat rises in my cheeks again. "Sorry again," I say sheepishly, and his eyes twinkle.

"Great, that makes me very happy," he says. "I'm glad I caught you at the beginning of tonight's events. It's a good opportunity for you to make some contacts. I'll try to find Dr. Jacobs and introduce you later since you'll be working closely together. But watch for my assistant, Kelly, to contact you on Monday. They'll get all the details of your transfer worked out with the HR department. I'd like you to start with us as soon as we can make it happen so once it's time to start the trial, you'll already have your feet under you."

"Carson, this is amazing," I sputter. "I mean, I can't thank you enough, really. This is an incredible opportunity."

"You've earned the chance. And I'm sure you'll do an excellent job," Carson says. "That's why I ambushed you. I wanted to make sure you could take advantage of this time to make some connections."

"Yeah, absolutely," I say, still stunned, but at the same time, my brain is spinning with ideas.

Just then, a voice comes over the PA system, politely asking us to take our seats, as the speeches will be starting soon, followed by dinner. Carson claps me on the shoulder. "Alright, Aleks, Let's go find our tables. I'll make sure to find you later to introduce you around."

Following him through the crowd of beautiful, glittering people, I shake my head, thinking about what an insane day this has been. I started out feeling like garbage after being ghosted, but I've now been given what could literally be the greatest opportunity of my career. It's crazy how the universe works sometimes. I can't wait to tell Josie—maybe she's right about all her metaphysical stuff after all.

Carson and I find our tables easily, as the *Sasquatch* has sent a sizeable group this evening. I already know several people at my table, and Carson is next to us with several more players and coaches. Our table is making polite small talk as one of the serving staff fills our wineglasses when a woman takes to the stage and begins introducing the keynote speaker, listing an impressive number of accomplishments. I admit, I groan inwardly as she lists his many credentials because it sounds like this guy will probably be some kind of pencil-necked geek who has no idea about hockey and can't tell one end of the stick from the other. I sincerely hope that's not the case, especially since I'm going to be spending a lot of time with this person soon.

A moment later, my mouth goes dry, and the bottom drops out of my stomach. I squint my eyes and then shake my head in a vain attempt to clear it because I can't possibly be seeing what I think I am. The man who has just walked out onto the stage... the person with whom I'm going to be spending many, many hours in the very near future, the esteemed and respected Dr. Benjamin Jacobs, is none other than my hookup from last night: Ben.

CHAPTER 9
Ben

It's just before 6:00 p.m. when the car sent for me arrives at the hotel where the gala is being held. For a second, I feel like a celebrity walking the red carpet. Due to the large number of sports celebs in attendance tonight, there are even a few paparazzi hanging around, but a random doctor doesn't warrant much excitement, so I just keep a neutral expression on my face and make my way into the hotel.

I had texted Nadia and Irena that I was on my way, so they're both waiting for me inside the ballroom after I get through security and check my coat.

"Oh, Dr. Ben, I'm so grateful you agreed to step in tonight!" Irena exclaims, wrapping her arms around me in a crushing hug. "I know you hate doing this stuff, but thank you so very much," she whispers in my ear.

"You're welcome, Irena. Thanks for asking me."

I give her an extra squeeze and turn to Nadia, who wraps me up in her own warm hug.

"Thank you, Benny. You know how much I appreciate you helping Irena out," she whispers.

"It's nothing," I say to her, and she takes a step back and holds on to my shoulders, one eyebrow raised.

"It's not nothing, and you know it. We appreciate you." She gives me a fond smile.

"Ben, why don't you go mingle for a little bit. I'll come and snag you about ten minutes before it's time for you to go on. Is that okay?" Irena asks.

I nod, trying to will my roiling stomach to calm down. "Sure."

Nadia tucks her hand into my arm. "Let's go get you a drink," she says. "Just one to take the edge off."

I look down at her and nod, although I'm not sure putting alcohol into my nervous stomach is the best plan, but I decide to roll with it. She leads me over to the bar at the side of the beautifully decorated ballroom, where she orders me a whiskey and ginger ale, and I finally crack a smile as I overhear her asking the bartender to go heavy on the ginger ale. Nadi knows me well.

A few moments later, she hands me my drink and takes a sip of her own. I give her a grateful smile. "Thanks for babysitting me, Nadi. I wish you didn't have to though. Christ, if I fuck up a speech, the only thing getting hurt is my ego. No patients to even worry about, and I'm a damn mess."

She rolls her eyes and waves her hand in the air. "Don't be ridiculous. Hanging out with you isn't babysitting. And you know as well as I do, Doctor, that fear of public speaking is a legitimate thing. Stop beating yourself up and drink. The ginger ale should help settle your tummy, and when you're done with the speech, I'll make sure you get a real drink." She waggles her eyebrows at me, which earns her a laugh, even though my gut is still in knots.

"Does that count as bribing me, I wonder?"

She arches a brow. "Benjamin Jacobs, I didn't raise three children into functioning adults without learning a thing or two. Now, I see Irena waving at us. Let's go get this shit taken care of!"

"Right," I say, downing the last swallow before following her up to where Irena is standing at the front of the room beside the giant Christmas tree.

"Okay, are you ready?" she says, reaching out with both hands and grasping onto my arms. Most of the guests have taken their seats or are at least heading in that direction, so I know it's go time. I close my eyes briefly, trying to focus on the moment and doing some of the deep-breathing exercises I use whenever I have to speak publicly. Not that any of the techniques ever work all that well, but I still try all the tricks, and I'm usually able to get through it without having a panic attack.

As Irena walks out onto the small stage, my heart races, blood thrumming in my ears and my palms sweating. She lists off my credentials for this room full of athletes and other sports types, most of whom won't have a clue what any of them mean. When she calls my name, I take one last deep breath and step out onto the stage, making my way to the podium as polite applause fills the room.

"Thank you so much, Ben. You're going to kill it," she whispers in my ear before stepping back with a beaming smile.

I swallow hard to keep my voice from cracking and take a quick look around the room. I can only see the first couple of tables in front of me, but I do notice a couple of doctors I've met in the past. Reed Morrow is an ER doc I've known for many years, and as I meet his eyes, he gives me a friendly smile. I've talked with him before about my issues with public speaking, and it does help to have a friendly face in the audience to focus on. Taking one last deep, cleansing breath, I paste a smile on my face and start talking. "Good evening, everyone. Thanks for having me tonight..."

As normally happens, once I start the actual speech, I'm able to find a kind of rhythm. Since I've presented this speech once before, I find my groove faster than usual, and before too long, I finish up to another round of polite applause. I exit stage left to find Nadia waiting for me with a huge hug and a flute of champagne.

"Perfectly done, as usual." She smiles. "Now, I want you to relax and enjoy your evening. And Ben, thank you again."

I shake out my arms and roll my head on my shoulders for a second, allowing the tension to bleed out of me before taking the champagne flute from her, pushing down the urge to shoot it like tequila. "You're welcome, Nadi. It wasn't too bad tonight. But I'm real fucking glad it's over."

Dinner is about to be served, so I stick with Nadia as she leads me to the table we're sharing with several other medical professionals. Reed, my unwitting savior during the speech, is there, so I get a chance to thank him for serving as my focal point during the speech. He's amused and very gracious about the whole thing. As we make polite conversation and enjoy the surprisingly good food, I glance around the ballroom to see which sporting celebrities are in attendance. There are several tables filled with players and executives from both the NHL and the NFL. I also clock folks from Major League Soccer teams from several West Coast cities. I'm pleased to see how many people from the professional leagues have shown up tonight; it seems like more than in the past. A few years ago, there's no way this room would have been full of this many hockey and football players and team executives. It's taken a long time, but hopefully, maybe, people are starting to pull their heads out of the sand about the dangers of head injuries in sports.

As we finish dinner, the adrenaline rush from my speech finally runs out, and I find myself yawning.

"God, Ben, you look like you need to go home and curl up in bed for a few hours," Reed teases, and I laugh.

"I was up late last night, and I'm beat. I think I'm probably going to ditch out of here early and do exactly that." We make small talk for a while longer before I excuse myself and start making my way toward the coat check area. I cannot wait to get home and slide into my bed. I just wish I wasn't going to be alone. It would be so nice to have a warm body to snuggle with tonight to celebrate my small victory over my phobia and the success of this event. Against my will, my mind flashes back to last night and how incredible Aleks felt curled up against me.

Goddammit. Gritting my teeth, I shove that thought aside. Last night was a one-off. And there are plenty of reasons it wouldn't be a good idea, even without the history between our fathers. For one thing, while the sex was amazing, the fact is Aleks Warren is a *lot* younger than me. I'll just add that onto the list of reasons I should not be sparing this guy a second thought.

As I'm almost to the door, I notice Carson Wells, the Sasquatch GM, heading toward me. He's a good-looking guy, tall and slim, with dark hair. Very bookish-looking, with a quiet confidence that seeps out of his pores, making him very attractive to be around. He's been straightforward and honest while we worked with our legal reps over the past few weeks, and he was calm and unflappable even when it looked like the players' union might torpedo the entire plan to get the helmets into live gameplay. I like him a lot.

"Dr. Jacobs, hi. I'm glad I caught you before you left," he says with a polite smile.

I shake his extended hand. "Call me Ben, please, since we'll be seeing more of each other soon," I reply, and he grins.

"Great, then please call me Carson. I think of Mr. Wells as my father." We both chuckle before he continues. "I was hoping you might have a couple of minutes so I could introduce you to someone?" Carson asks, and I nod politely, even though I'm dying to get home to bed.

"Of course. That would be great."

"Perfect. He's just over this way." He turns to lead us toward the far side of the ballroom. The crowd thins out enough for us to walk side by side, and he fills me in as we weave through the tables.

"So, nothing is official yet, of course, but I thought this would be a good opportunity for you to meet the person who'll be running point for the helmet project from our side. We're stealing him from our AHL affiliate."

"Ah, got called up to the show, did he?" I quip, and he chuckles.

"You could say that. Aleks has been the equipment team lead for the Emerald City Eagles for the past year and a half. I think he'll be a great fit for this project. He's got an exceptional hockey mind, even though he's never played at the pro level. He comes from a huge family of top-level players though, so he's well aware of what the guys will need and what questions they'll have."

Suddenly, my head starts to swim, and the palms of my hands get sweaty. *Did he say Aleks? Someone who doesn't play the game but comes from a big hockey family. No... It can't be...*

He leads me over to a huddle of giant-sized Sasquatch players. They're all laughing about something, their attention focused on one man who's much shorter than the rest. One of the players—I think it's Rylan Collings, their team captain—is standing directly in front of the smaller man, doing something with the man's bow tie, I think. It's hard to tell what's going on, but there's a lot of laughter and jeering from the other guys, and Rylan's face is bright red. Everyone seems to be having fun though. As we approach, Rylan takes a step back from the shorter man, who immediately drops to the ground with an exaggerated flourish, one knee bent, and bows before the team captain in a theatrical display of worship. Then, he clasps his hands clasped over his heart and turns his face up toward Rylan with a wide grin. When we're finally close enough to see him clearly, I have to stifle my gasp as the room spins around me.

Because, sure enough, the person Carson was raving about, the person I'm going to be working closely with on a project critical to my career, the person who is currently on his *knees*, flirting shamelessly with the gorgeous team captain of the Seattle Sasquatch, is none other than the man I hooked up with and ditched last night. Aleks Warren.

"Dr. Benjamin Jacobs, I'd like you to meet Aleks Warren," Carson says with a gracious smile.

Aleks scrambles to his feet, hurriedly brushing off the knees of his pants before he turns around. His eyes widen as he reaches up to adjust his bow tie, which is slightly crooked, I note with a sense of satisfaction. *Guess Rylan Collings isn't perfect at everything.*

He swallows hard when he sees me, but otherwise, there's no outward sign he even recognizes me, which feels like a knife to the chest. Mix that with my irrational jealousy over how cozy he seems to be acting with Rylan Collings, and I feel like a confused teenager.

"Hi, Dr. Jacobs," he says with a friendly smile, extending his hand. "Great to meet you."

"Hello," I say politely. I take his hand and try to ignore the shot of electricity that shoots up my arm as our palms meet.

"Aleks has agreed to come on board with the Sasquatch to be the point person for the helmet project," Carson says. "Although it looks like you and Rylan have been doing some work on neck protection?" He grins mischievously.

Aleks blushes, and Rylan lets out a good-natured laugh, throwing his arm around Aleks' shoulders. I literally have to bite back a growl. *What the hell is wrong with me? I'm not a jealous person.* Not to mention the fact that Rylan Collings, as far as I know, is straight as a goddamn arrow. But some primal force inside me wants to rip that meaty arm off Aleks's shoulders and tear Rylan fucking Collings limb from limb for daring to flirt with Aleks. Because he's *mine.*

"Just making sure young Aleks here is wearing all his equipment, including his bow tie, properly." Rylan grins at his GM. "Can't be too careful, y'know, boss."

Carson chuckles. "Glad you're all so keen on proper equipment protocols. It will come in useful during the helmet trial."

I wouldn't be able to recount the next few minutes of conversation if someone held a gun to my head. I can only hope I didn't act so weird that Carson or anyone else picked up on it. All I know is after a couple of minutes of polite small talk, I make my excuses and hightail it out of that party as fast as humanly possible. I don't even stop to say good night to Nadia and Irena, texting them from my Uber instead, my chest constricted with anxiety. Relief floods over me when I finally get back to my condo, but as soon as I close the door behind me, I lean back against it with a loud groan. "What the fuck am I going to do now?" I mutter to myself as the weight of this fucked-up situation hits me full force.

CHAPTER 10
Aleks

I let out a loud groan as I drag my eyes open on Sunday morning. My phone is pinging incessantly with Josie's individual tone, and she's going to be pissed if I ignore her, but I barely got any sleep. I tossed and turned for hours after getting home, unable to decide if I should be happy about my new job or if I should be freaking the fuck out. Obviously, it's going to be slightly awkward working with the guy who fucked me and ran a couple of nights ago, but as I thought more about it last night, I realized that's not the only problem I'm facing.

My dad refuses to believe CTE exists. He played in the NHL for many years; he was what they used to call an enforcer. One of the last of his kind, his job was to protect his teammates with brute force. That kind of player is no longer a part of the game, but back when my dad played, it was serious as fuck. If any of the big scorers took a hit they didn't like or there was a missed call on a penalty, the enforcer took care of it, which usually meant some unlucky guy from the other team was gonna get the shit kicked out of him.

Just to add to my fun and games this weekend, today is our regular family lunch slash hockey game. Because my dad is... well... an over-the-top kind of guy, when they built their house, he had his own mini hockey rink built. Yeah, that's right. Literally, my family has a private hockey rink in a separate building on their huge lakefront property.

We try to get together every few months to pass the puck around in a friendly game. My brothers aren't often around during the season, but my sister and her boyfriend are usually there. Josie often comes, and my dad's always got a few of his old random hockey buddies around who are happy to jump back onto the ice.

As a teenager, I dreaded these command perfor-mances, but as I've gotten older, I've realized they're actually kind of special. My dad, as much as he drives me crazy, really does love having us all together on the ice. After she retired from the Olympic figure skating team, my mom coached younger skaters for a long time, so that extremely OTT ice rink has always gotten a lot of use.

The problem I need to solve, before seeing dad today, is how I should approach the topic of my new job, and it's a lot more complicated than it should be.

The NHL, like most other giant western businesses, is run by a cabal of older white men. My dad has worked with NHL executives and owners since shortly after he retired, and he fits right into the old boys' club. Despite all evidence to the contrary, none of them will acknowledge CTE exists, or if it does, they deny that hockey has any role in causing it. Their generation believes any guy who doesn't bounce back up after a wickedly hard hit is just weak. It doesn't matter what the science says or how my dad needs two hands to count how many of his fellow enforcers are either brain damaged or gone, my father and the NHL stubbornly insist on keeping their heads firmly buried in the sand.

When Dad finds out I've been brought up to the "big leagues" only to run an initiative to protect players from this "imaginary condition," his reaction is going to be interesting.

Reaching for the phone, I call Josie instead of texting because this situation definitely calls for bottomless mimosas, and an hour later, we're sliding into a booth at our favorite brunch joint. By some stroke of magical luck, we didn't even have to wait for a table, so I'm hoping that's a good omen for today's family gathering.

"So, spill," Josie says after we've both ordered and have our mimosas in hand. "You sounded stressed on the phone, and the bags under your eyes are telling me you didn't sleep, but I don't think it's because you were having too much fun."

"Ugh. Jo, it's so fucked-up. I should be throwing a damn party right now, but the universe is conspiring against me, I swear!" So much has gone on over the last couple of days since I left her at the bar on Friday night, we're almost finished our eggs bennys and on our third mimosa by the time I've caught her up. Once I finish, she leans back and blows out a breath.

"Dude, you were not kidding when you said this was complicated," she chuckles, and I toss a balled-up napkin at her.

"Yeah, thanks. But you're supposed to tell me what I should do, not laugh at me!"

Smiling, she leans forward again, taking another sip from her champagne flute. "Well, you need to accept that position because you'd be an idiot not to. You and Dr. McSexy Pants are just going to have to be grown-ups about the situation. You don't owe him anything but professional courtesy, especially since the asshole ghosted you. It'll be awkward for a couple of days, but it'll pass. And as for your dad..." She pauses and chews on her lip for a moment. She knows I have a difficult relationship with my dad, but she also knows from personal experience that underneath his super-macho, toxic-man façade, Kent Warren is a good person. It makes her a good sounding board for me when I have issues with him because she knows him so well.

"I think it will be better if you just tell him right away. If he finds out you've been promoted from someone else, he's not only going to be pissed about the job itself, but he'll be hurt that you didn't tell him. And when your dad is pissed and hurt, it's not great for anyone."

"Pffft. Yeah. I knew you'd say that," I mutter dejectedly. "I know I have to tell him, but I really don't feel like listening to him rant about how doctors and the 'woke left' are trying to change sports."

Josie nods sympathetically as she finishes the last of her mimosa. "I get it, hon. But here's the thing. Your dad really does adore you. I know you find it hard to believe, but it's true." She shoots me a mischievous grin. "Maybe tell him when you first arrive so you can have a couple of drinks early in the day before you drive home?"

I snort a laugh. "Um, yeah, great strategy, Jo. Hey, you know," I say as an idea occurs to me. "It would be waaaay easier if you came with me. How about it?" I give her my best puppy dog eyes, hoping she'll take pity on me and tag along as a distraction.

I expect her to make excuses right away, but when I see her thinking about it, I crank up the pressure by sprinkling a little guilt into the mix. "You know it's been ages since you've seen them. Plus, if you're there, it will take some heat off me. And I need you with me so I don't sit around and mope about my sexy doctor. Please, please, please?"

I clasp my hands in front like I'm praying, and she rolls her eyes.

"Ugh, okay, fine, you've successfully guilted me into it, Manipulator-Boy."

I grin happily. "Oh, thank you so much, lovey! Having you there will make this so much easier. Plus, they really do miss you. They've asked about you the last couple of times I've seen them."

She waves her hand. "Yeah, yeah, I've already said I'll come with you. You can ease up on the guilt now."

I just shoot her another jubilant grin before we make plans for me to pick her up in a couple of hours and then part ways.

I wasn't exactly joking when I said I wanted her to help distract me from thinking about Ben. Even though I said it as a joke, I'm pretty sure she can see right through me and can tell that I'm low-key obsessing about him. Fuck, I have no idea how I'm going to be able to work with the guy without walking around with a super-hard dick all day long. *Sigh*. I guess we're gonna find out real soon.

When it's time to get ready, I force my ass into a pair of skinny black jeans and a soft blue polo shirt, throwing a set of warm-ups into a bag for the game.

After picking Josie up from her little house in Queen Anne, we head east to my parents' big house on Lake Washington. Even though Josie's with me, I'm still nervous about how my dad will react when I give him the details of my new job. I imagine that if we had a normal relationship, I'd be excited to tell him about my promotion. Maybe he'd be impressed or even happy for me landing this kind of high-profile, important job. But my dad and I have never had a normal relationship.

Being both the youngest and the smallest of his children, I've always felt like a bit of an afterthought in my family. I've never doubted that they all love me, but I was never the kid they bragged about. When I was younger, I remember hearing my parents gush to their friends about how well Mike and Brad were doing on their respective junior teams, and what an incredible hockey player Christine is, and on and on.

My accomplishments have always been more on the low-key side. Doing well at the science fair or bringing home a good grade on a math test never really compared to winning state championships or making the US Olympic team.

Pulling into the long, curved driveway, Jo and I hop out of my red Tesla and head to the huge, arched double front doors, which are decorated for the season with a matching pair of stunning live wreaths, complete with little sparkly twinkle lights. It might not be exactly my style, but no one can argue my mom's impeccable taste. The house always looks like something out of a magazine, especially around the holidays.

I always have to remind myself that I don't need to ring the bell when I come here. Even though this is where I grew up, it's never really felt like home to me. My loft in Capitol Hill has always felt more comfortable than this fancy mansion.

As we walk into the house, the sound of an NFL football broadcast reaches me from my dad's den. It's too early for hockey games to be on, and football has always been his second favorite obsession. Jo and I ditch our coats and boots at the door and head to the kitchen, where we find my mom and my sister chatting. To my surprise, my brother Brad is leaning against the large kitchen island, his arms crossed over his chest.

"Hey, what are you doing here?" I ask. He plays for the Florida Jaguars, so he's not on the West Coast much during the season. His twin, Mike, plays in Los Angeles, so we see him a lot more often. Brad comes over and wraps a meaty arm around my neck, holding me down to give me a noogie. Obviously, I *love* when he's in town.

"Hey, lil' bro! Don't I even get a 'nice to see you'? What, are you not happy to see your big brother for some reason?" I love my siblings, but Brad has always had more of an edge than the other two. Since I came out a few years ago, I've wondered if part of the reason is homophobia. I don't like to think that way, but it's possible. The world of pro hockey isn't exactly the most pro-LGBTQIA+ environment.

"Fuck off, let go of me," I mutter, pushing at him. He releases me, and after giving Josie a big hug, he grabs a handful of grapes from the bowl on the counter before disappearing down the hall, probably to hang out with Dad.

"What is he doing here?" I ask my sister, Christine, who's retaken her seat on a barstool at the island after squealing and giving Jo a huge hug.

Josie and my mom are chatting in front of the professional-grade, stainless steel range while Mom stirs something that smells like her spaghetti sauce, so I grab the stool beside Chrissy.

"They're playing in Vegas tomorrow night, so he got permission to come out early. He's flying down there in the morning," she answers.

"Aleksandr," my mom says, coming around the island to hug me. She's already enlisted Josie to babysit the sauce while she comes to greet me. "How are you, love?" She gives me a perfunctory kiss on the cheek, and before I get a chance to answer, she turns back around and says something to Christine before disappearing into the large pantry. Christine slides off her barstool and grabs a stick of butter that's sitting on the counter to soften and tossing it into a bowl before going in search of spices for the garlic bread.

My mom's family is originally from Russia, but she doesn't have many fond memories of living there. They moved to Italy when she was very small, so when she cooks, which isn't terribly often, it's usually Italian food. I'll give her credit though; her spaghetti sauce and her lasagna are top-notch. I imagine she's whipped up this special dinner because Brad's here. Mostly during the hockey season, our family gatherings involve takeout.

"So, where's your man today?" I ask Christine. Her boyfriend, Thomas, is usually here for family dinners, although I know my mom stresses him out when she starts hinting that he needs to propose to my sister. Honestly, I'm not sure Christine wants to marry Thomas. He's a nice guy, but they don't seem to have much in common.

"He's in LA this week. Said to tell everyone hello," she replies without looking up from the buttery garlic mixture.

My mom comes back into the kitchen, and the four of us make boring small talk until Josie appears beside me and pinches my arm.

"Ow!" I exclaim, rubbing the sore spot and glaring at her.

"It's time. Let's go talk to your dad," she says with an arched eyebrow.

Both Chrissy and my mom give me curious looks, but I wave them off. "I need to talk to Dad, but I'll fill you in after," I say, taking a deep breath and squaring my shoulders as I head down the hall with Jo right behind me.

We step into the big den with wood-paneled walls and French doors that open onto a huge stone patio facing the lake, and I immediately feel small, as I always do in this room. A giant TV takes up most of one wall, and comfortable chairs and couches are scattered around the room. A different wall is taken up with hockey memorabilia, including his two Stanley Cup rings and various other trophies and framed jerseys, et cetera. Dad is sitting on one couch while Brad is lying on another, tossing a ball in the air and catching it as he keeps one eye on the football game. They're discussing something about Brad's team, but when we enter the room, they stop talking.

"Aleks, good to see you, son," Dad says, but his eyes light up when Josie comes into the room after me.

"Josie!" he exclaims, getting out of his chair and wrapping Jo in a huge hug. Even though my dad and I aren't close and he drives me crazy a lot of the time, I know he's a good person, simply because of how he is with Josie. My parents both love her as much as they love any of their biological kids, and I couldn't be more grateful for that, because love was something Jo never had before she became part of our lives.

After Dad's caught up with Jo a bit, he turns to me. "How are things at the rink these days, son?"

"Yeah, you taking good care of all the jockstraps?" Brad snorts. "Making sure they're all hand-washed and shined up nice?"

I shoot him a dirty look. "Fuck off, asshole." I shouldn't even respond. Of course, everyone in this room knows full well that cleaning players' jock straps is *not* part of my job. But for some reason, my thirty-six-year-old brother seems to think it's hilarious to tease me about having to clean the players' underwear.

"Things are good, Dad," I say, not bothering to look at Brad. "Actually, I've got some good news." I swallow. *May as well jump in with both feet.*

"Great!" he says enthusiastically, and a little spark of hope flares to life in my chest. Maybe this won't be too bad.

"So, I was at a fundraiser last night with a bunch of guys from the Sasquatch, and Carson Wells was there."

"Is that right?" Dad says. "Good, I'm glad they're inviting you to some of that frou-frou fundraising shit. Good to get your name in front of people who make decisions."

"Right. Anyway, Carson pulled me aside to tell me about a new project the Sasquatch is going to be involved in. He asked me to come over and manage it for them."

This gets my dad's attention, as I knew it would. "Really?" he asks. "What's the project?"

"Well, it's still not official yet, so I can't tell you everything, but it's going to be gathering data for a doctor who's researching CTE. I'm really excited about it."

"Wait a minute. You mean to tell me the Sasquatch are actually encouraging one of these whack-job doctors to come in and mess around with shit? In the middle of the season? The GM wants this to happen?" he barks rapid-fire questions at me.

"Well, yeah, Dad. There are a lot of people who feel like the game could be—and should be—a lot safer. I know you don't agree, but maybe the league is starting to realize the science is pretty undeniable." I swallow down my frustration. This isn't the first conversation like this I've had with my father.

"Sure, sure, but I still don't see the point of it." He waves his hand dismissively. "It's not like there's any solid proof that hits in hockey are directly related to this CTS or whatever they're calling it these days. I'm very curious to see how Sasquatch coach feels about you guys fucking around with his players' equipment." *My father, ladies and gentlemen. Challenging scientific fact with toxic masculinity wherever he can find it.*

I fight not to roll my eyes. "It's CT*E*, Dad, and I don't know how the coach feels about it, but Wells is pumped, and apparently, the ownership group is as well."

"Seems like a waste of fuckin' resources if you ask me. The Sasquatch are on top of their division in their first year. I swear, if this so-called 'safety project' fucks up their game, the shit'll hit the fan." He uses air quotes around "safety project," and I have to bite my lip to keep my mouth shut. This ridiculous idea of CTE being some kind of devious plot has been part of my dad's belief system for as long as people have known about it. Josie and I exchange glances.

"Dad, I don't know what back-channel conversations have been happening, but I assume Carson got whatever go-ahead he needed from the league. Can you at least admit this is a great opportunity for me? I mean, I'm getting pulled up from the *Eagles* to handle this for him. It's kind of a big deal."

Fucking fuckity fuck. Why, why, why *am I constantly seeking this man's approval?* I should just let this damn conversation die. I know this job is a big deal. I'm a grown-ass man. I should not need his validation to feel proud of myself.

"Sure, son, it sounds like a good project for you. You'll do well with the nerd herd. You always have." He gets up and walks over to where Brad is now standing by the door and throws an arm over his shoulders.

"Personally, I think it's best to leave all that kind of crap to the nerds, right, son?" he says to Brad. "You got games to win, and I wanna see some big plays from you tomorrow night, you hear me?" he says, guiding my brother out of the room.

I roll my eyes as Josie and I trail after them down the hallway. "Why the hell do I even bother?" I mutter, and Jo grabs my hand, squeezing it comfortingly. She doesn't say anything, but she doesn't have to. What's to say? I just need to accept that there's nothing I'll ever do that'll earn me his respect. I just wish I didn't care so fucking much.

CHAPTER 11
Aleks

I don't talk much more to my dad or Brad during lunch, but that's not unusual. Instead, I chat with Jo, my mom, and Christine while my father and brother have their own little boys' club meeting down at the other end of the table. I feel like they should be wearing signs around their necks: "No Girls (or Gays) Allowed."

Once we clean up from lunch, it's game time. I swear, if I thought there was any possible way I could leave early and skip the so-called "friendly game" entirely, I would, but I know I'd never hear the end of it, so it's probably better to tough it out.

The low, steady hum of the rink's refrigeration system echoes through the air as I sit on the bench, lacing up my skates. The artificial lighting casts a cool glow on the ice, adding to the charged atmosphere. It's always like this before these "friendly" family games. As much as I'm not really up for this today, these games aren't nearly as bad as they used to be. When I was growing up, I dreaded them. Even though I didn't get the star athlete genes, I'm still pretty competitive, and being the lone nonplayer in a house full of exceptional athletes isn't a fun experience. I wrestled for years with the weight of my family's expectations on my shoulders, knowing there was no way I'd ever be able to measure up. I've always loved hockey, so it was heartbreaking to know I'd never be as good as my brothers and sister, but once I figured out how much I love the strategy part of the game and figuring out the big picture, I stopped caring about these games quite as much, which allowed me to enjoy them more. But even now, those old feelings of inadequacy still find me sometimes.

Beside me, Josie adjusts her gear with focused determination. Jo is enough of a natural athlete that she can keep up with me, but of course, everyone else skates rings around both of us.

We always draw straws for teams, and this time, it ends up being me, Christine, and Mom against Dad, Brad, and Jo. Brad, ever the asshole, just can't resist stirring up some shit as we enter the face-off circle. "Watch out, little brother. Don't want to mess up that important job of yours," he taunts.

I try to ignore him, but my frustration level is already high, and I can't stop myself from glaring at him. "Just focus on the game, asshole."

Josie skates up to me and murmurs low enough so only I can hear, "Don't let him get to you. That's what he wants."

I nod, but I'm still pissed off, so I take a deep breath, trying to focus. Naturally, I lose the face-off to Brad, who passes it to my dad, who controls it effortlessly. The two of them pass it back and forth between them, easily deking around both me and my mom as we try to defend our net. Christine manages to get in the way of a quick wrist shot by Dad, saving a goal. The competitive nature of my family is out in full fucking force today, and as the game continues, the intensity builds.

Brad intercepts a pass from Mom that was meant for me, and he quickly maneuvers around Christine, meeting my eyes with a smirk before burying the puck in the net. By this point, their team is so far ahead of us we stop keeping score. It's got Christine riled up because these games aren't supposed to be ultra-competitive, but Brad is really fucking with the vibe today.

A few minutes later, I'm back in the face-off circle again, this time against my dad. I'm determined to prove myself, and this time, I win the face-off. Instead of passing, I weave between Brad and Josie, taking my shot without hesitation and squeaking it into the net as Brad hurls himself on the ice in a vain attempt to block it.

"Jesus, Bradley, calm the fuck down," Dad says to him, eyebrows raised. "Your coach will have my balls if you get hurt during a family game of shinny."

Brad doesn't say anything, just seems to double down on his shitty attitude. He's always been edgier and even more competitive than my other siblings, but today's attitude is too much, even for him. I have no idea what's going on with him, but clearly, something is under his skin.

Even Dad can see something's up with him, and he pulls Brad aside a few minutes later, talking to him quietly.

"The fuck is going on with Thing 2 today?" Josie asks me quietly, using the silly nickname she has for Mike and Brad. Brad is Thing 2 because he's a few minutes younger than Mike.

"No idea," I answer. "But at least it's got my Dad's mind off me." Jo and I watch as Dad tries reasoning with my brother, but it seems like it's not helping much today. It's like he's on some kind of mission to ruin the game for the family. His face is flushed with anger, and I can just about see the steam coming out of his ears as he listens to our dad, who's probably ripping him a new one. Dad's not particularly known for his soft touch when it comes to coaching—or anything else, really—which is why he was strongly encouraged *not* to pursue coaching after he retired. He's too much of a pit bull for a job that occasionally requires a soft touch.

After their conversation, we resume playing, although we're all a little distracted now that it's clear something's bugging Brad. A few minutes later, I get a chance when I intercept a pass meant for Josie from my dad. Determination fueling me, I dodge past my brother's attempt to haul me down, which would have really pissed Dad off if he'd been successful. As I reach the net, I get that slightly surreal feeling I always do when I'm about to score a goal. I hear the sound of my skates on the ice, and I'm conscious of my heart beating in my chest. With a swift flick of my wrist, I send the puck across the ice like a bullet. Brad again dives for it, trying to make the save, but it finds its mark in the corner of the net.

"Yeah!" I shout, clutching my fist and raising my stick in the air. Mom and Chrissy come over to exchange high fives, but when I glance over, I see Brad is still lying on the ice. He's rolled onto his back, and he's just lying there, staring up at the ceiling. Dad gets a worried look on his face, and he and my mom skate over to where Brad's lying. Josie and I follow right behind them.

"Bradley, you alright, son?" Dad calls before he reaches him. Brad responds by sitting up and shaking his head.

"You know what, guys? I'm just not fuckin' into this today. Sorry, Dad."

My dad's brow creases with concern. "It's fine, son. Why don't we call it for today, if your heart's not in it."

My own eyebrows shoot up into my hairline. Normally my dad is fanatical about playing these games through to the end, so he must be pretty worried about whatever's going on with Brad if he's willing to call the game early. I exchange a glance with my sister as Dad helps Brad up and we head toward the benches.

My parents both hang back with Brad as Josie, Christine, and I take our skates off and head back to the main house.

"Do you know what's up with him?" I ask my sister when the three of us get back to the kitchen.

"I think his game is in the toilet and he's really stressed about it. The Jaguars suck again this year, and I think maybe he's starting to realize he's closer to the end of his career than the beginning. He hasn't got one goddamn clue about what he's going to do after hockey, and he's freaking out."

"Really?" I ask. "What makes you think that's the problem?"

"He asked me earlier how I knew when it was the right time to retire," she says, grabbing an orange out of the fruit bowl on the counter. "I almost laughed at him since it's not exactly the same thing. It's not like I was making any money on the national team, so as soon as it stopped being something I looked forward to and I was over thirty, I knew it was time. For guys like Brad and Mike, it's a different calculation." She shrugs. "I think that's why he came here to talk to Dad before their game tomorrow."

"Oh. Do you think he's considering retiring before the season ends?" I ask, and she shrugs again.

"He didn't say. I'd be surprised though. He'll probably wait until the end of this season. But what's going on with you? What was the big talk you had to have with Dad earlier?" she asks.

So I tell her about the helmet project and my new job, and she's appropriately excited for me. I don't tell her that my brand-new coworker is someone who I hooked up with only a few nights ago, though. Some things are on a need-to-know basis only, and my older, extremely level-headed, and totally responsible sister does *not* need to know this particular detail about my life.

A few minutes later, my parents and Brad come back in. Brad seems to be back to his normal self, but

Josie and I exchange glances and wordlessly decide it's time to head out. I want to be fresh for this week since it promises to be a big one.

As we say goodbye to my family, Brad gives me an unusually big hug. "Good luck with the new job, little bro," he says. "And, uh, sorry I was a dick today. Just going through a rough patch."

"Thanks, Brad," I say, noticing Josie's raised eyebrows. It's definitely not normal for Brad to apologize for anything and even less normal for him to admit to anything that could be construed as weakness, like "going through a rough patch." Who knows, maybe my older brother is finally growing up.

As Josie and I head back across the lake, excitement about my new job courses through me. I can't believe this week could be the start of my NHL career, something I've dreamed about for my entire life. Sure, it would be nice if my father was a bit more excited on my behalf, but it doesn't matter. Without being overdramatic, I need to focus on the fact that this week could literally be the start of my dreams coming true, and I am here for all of it.

CHAPTER 12
Ben

Monday morning, I arrive at the Sasquatch offices, located in a beautiful, spacious area adjacent to their rink in downtown Seattle. I'm so damn nervous I'm sweating like a snowman in a sauna as the elevator takes me up to the executive area. All I can do is hope no one can tell I haven't been able to sleep in days. I can't fucking get Aleks Warren out of my head. Seeing him at the fundraiser on Saturday night set off my anxiety, and I can't stop imagining the worst possible scenarios of what could come from working together. On Saturday night, when Carson "introduced" us, he acted like we'd never met before, which was understandable. But as we stood around making small talk with the group, I noticed him stealing the occasional glance at me, and the look on his face was anything but warm and welcoming.

He's certainly within his rights to be pissed at the way I ditched him the other night; it was a real dick move. But even though I have no idea how I'm going to handle things with him, I can't bring myself to regret that night. Fuck, it was amazing, and I've been replaying it every damn time I close my eyes, meaning sleep has been real hard to come by.

My weird, jealous reaction when I saw him goofing around with the Sasquatch players only confuses me more. I've never been a jealous guy, ever, and I have absolutely no claim to Aleks, so where the hell is the jealousy coming from? I don't know what kind of spell the man's cast on me, but it's powerful.

The team office is decked out for Christmas with all hockey-themed décor, including stockings made to look like skates hanging from the reception desk, each with a different NHL team logo and colors.

I make my way to Carson's office, where his assistant, an attractive young person sporting a *They/Them* pronoun button on the lapel of their gray pantsuit, shows me to the conference room, and my impression of Carson Wells shoots up another couple of levels. I like the way this team seems to legitimately walk the talk when it comes to diversity. The hockey-Christmas theme continues into the boardroom, where a Christmas tree sits in the corner of the room, a large wing-backed chair sitting beside it. There are stacks of presents under the tree, and on a small side table beside the chair is a stack of what looks like children's books.

After getting me set with a cup of coffee and pointing to the small plate of pastries on the counter at the back of the room, the assistant, whose name is Kelly, leaves, and I'm left to my own devices to wait for Aleks and Carson. I wander over to the tree, and I smile as I see the kids' books are a selection of hockey-themed holiday stories. The famous Canadian children's story *The Christmas Sweater,* is on the top of the pile. I'm thumbing through the old book, remembering when my mom used to read it to me as a kid sometimes when Aleks steps into the boardroom. He looks absolutely edible, even though the look on his face is impassive. His green eyes focus intently on me as we shake hands, but the hint of a smile crosses his face when he notices the book in my hands.

I'm about to take the bull by the horns and apologize for sneaking out on him a few nights ago when Carson enters the room. He's a commanding presence, even though he's young for his position. Tall and lean, he's wearing a perfectly tailored charcoal suit with a stunning royal blue dress shirt. His Patek Philippe watch peeks out from under his cuff as he shakes my hand first and then Aleks'. "Good morning, you two." He smiles widely when he sees me holding the old kids' book. "We're doing a kids' party here in a couple of nights, so we've got Santa's station all ready for him. That's a great choice in reading material you've picked up there." He grins, heading to the back counter to grab a coffee.

"I remember my mom reading it to me as a kid," I say. "A true Canadian classic."

Carson nods, his eyes warm. "Absolutely. You grew up in Canada?"

I nod. "Yeah, Saskatchewan. Spent many an afternoon playing hockey on backyard rinks outside of Saskatoon." We both chuckle. "Fuck, it was cold though."

"I bet," Carson laughs. "I'm Canadian too, although I'm a city kid. Grew up in Etobicoke, outside of Toronto."

Aleks' eyes ping-pong between us as Carson and I spend a few minutes reminiscing about our childhoods.

"I don't tend to advertise it, but my stepdad played in the league for years," I say. I have no idea why I'm sharing this with these two men. I rarely tell anyone I'm related to Bob, mostly because it's his story to share, not mine. I'm sure he doesn't want to be the poster boy for CTE, and given the nature of my research, people would make assumptions about my motives.

"Really?" Carson asks. "Who's your stepdad?"

"Bob Prescott," I say, and sure enough, Carson's reaction tells me he knows the story. His eyes widen slightly, and he darts his gaze to Aleks for a split second before focusing back on me. Aleks doesn't react.

"Oh," Carson says. "How is Bob doing these days? Last I heard, he had moved into a memory care facility?"

I nod. "He's doing fairly well. He was recently accepted into a drug trial that's had incredible results in other people, so we're very hopeful it will have a positive impact on him."

I turn to Aleks, who's wearing a look of confusion. "My stepdad played for almost twenty years in the league, but he was an enforcer. He's been in a memory care facility for a couple of years now, and we're certain his dementia is caused by CTE," I explain. "Although, as you know, that can't be confirmed until after someone passes away."

I can't help but wonder if Aleks' father has ever mentioned the incident to him since he would be too young to remember it himself. While it was a big topic of conversation around the league for a while, it happened so long ago that it's entirely possible Aleks only knows my dad's name as one of his father's many fighting partners. If Kent never talked to him about it, it's not hard to imagine that other people might not bring it up around him, thinking it might be embarrassing for him or something.

"Oh my god, I'm so sorry! I didn't know," Aleks says, some of the coldness in his bright green eyes melting away. "I recognize his name, but I didn't realize... You must know of my father, then. Kent Warren." His face doesn't show any hint that he knows the history between our fathers; there's only sympathy and compassion there. "It's so sad that so many of these big guys are affected by CTE. My dad's just been really lucky up until this point, I guess. He was an enforcer too."

I swallow hard and nod, noticing Carson gauging my reaction to Aleks' obvious ignorance. But I get that it's not his fault. "Yeah. I know of your dad. But like I said, Bob's doing alright these days, so we're staying optimistic." I give him a reassuring smile.

Carson clears his throat and steers the subject into safer territory. "We're doing a kids' party here in a couple of nights, which is why we've got Santa's station all ready for him," he says as we settle around the polished wood conference table. "You should think about joining us, Ben. A lot of players will be here, and most of the staff and their families."

"I'll think about it. Thanks for the invite," I say with a smile, not entirely convinced I want to hang out at a kids' Santa party, but who knows.

"So," Carson begins. "I'm excited to get moving forward on this project. And I'm so glad I could introduce you two the other night at the fundraiser. I have a really good feeling about this. I think we're going to be able to do some great things."

We jump right into the nuts and bolts of the meeting, discussing everything from how the helmets themselves will need to be cared for to the different ways the data needs to be managed. We're joined partway through the meeting by the team doctor and their PT and training staff. I've got answers for almost all the questions that come up, and Aleks is a big help when more specific questions are asked, and by the time we're done going through all the minutiae, the day has flown by.

After we finish up, I deliberately take my time as everyone begins to clear the room, until it's only Aleks and myself left. He turns to me once the door shuts behind the last person, his gaze impersonal, causing my stomach to clench uncomfortably.

Clearing my throat, I force myself to meet his eyes. "So, Aleks, I just wanted a quick word with you, if that's okay?"

"Of course. What can I help you with, Dr. Jacobs?" he asks. His voice is cool, the warmth he seemed to be feeling when we talked about my dad earlier apparently long gone.

"I, ah. Look, Aleks, I want to apologize for last week. Obviously, I had no idea that we would end up working together. If I'd known, I would have never—"

Aleks cuts me off by holding up his hand.

"Please don't say anything. We're grown-ups here. I think we both enjoyed ourselves, and as adults, I'm sure we can move on without it being a big deal, right?" he asks, his mouth pinched into a thin line. His icy tone stings, but I suppose I deserve it.

"Um, yes, right, Okay. Well, good, then. I just wanted to make sure things were, ah, okay between us. This project is incredibly important to me personally, as well as to the body of research on head injury."

"I understand," Aleks says. "It's important to me also. I want this project to be a success for many reasons, Dr. Jacobs, so you can rest easy knowing I'm going to do everything I can to make sure it goes flawlessly."

His words are devoid of emotion, but the ice in his eyes has melted again, and I can even see what I think is a spark of heat in them as he stares at me. God, all I can think about is jumping over the table and ripping his clothes off so I can fuck him senseless again, right here in the conference room.

But I fight back those totally unprofessional thoughts. This *has to* remain professional. The success of my project depends on us working together, and I refuse to jeopardize years' worth of work by my incredible team because I can't keep my dick in my pants. But Jesus Christ, there is something about Aleks Warren I can't resist. He's like a drug I could very easily get addicted to.

A few people in today's meeting asked Aleks how his father was doing, and he mentioned seeing him recently. I got the impression that he's close to his dad. Kent Warren is still very much part of the NHL, doing some kind of consulting with the league's president and team owners. I know he remains a CTE denier, so I'd been hoping this entire project could fly under his radar so he doesn't try to cause any problems for us. Of course, having his son in charge of the project means that's not going to happen.

I'm not even sure Kent Warren would know who I am, since my last name is different than Bob's, even though I'm pretty sure I met him as a young teen a few times. But as far as I know, once the hubbub died down after my dad retired, Kent never spoke publicly about it again. And I know he never contacted my dad to talk about it, so maybe it's possible he just forgot the whole thing, just let that big hit fade away into his memory with the hundreds of others he handed out over the course of his long career.

"Right, if that's all, then I'll see you tomorrow sometime," Aleks says, gathering his tablet and phone off the conference table.

"Yes, thanks. See you tomorrow," I say awkwardly, fighting the feeling of loss that settles into my chest. Which is dumb. *You can't lose something you've never had.*

He gives me a tight smile before heading out the door, leaving me alone in the empty conference room.

After getting back to my place, I sit on the couch, trying to watch TV, but I can't even concentrate on mindless reality shows. I should be thrilled this project is finally happening. It's been tons of blood, sweat, and tears by a lot of amazing people to get it to this point. It's a big accomplishment, and it could mean huge things for research into brain injury, which is the whole reason I went into this field in the first place.

But instead of celebrating, I feel like a pathetic loser. In a desperate move, I call Declan to see if he wants to meet for a drink, but unsurprisingly, he's out with Chloe, the girl from the bar on the night I met Aleks. So, I'm left to stew in my own juices.

What kind of fucking spell has Aleks cast on me that makes me think about him constantly? I've never been this obsessed with someone. *What the hell is happening to me?*

CHAPTER 13
Aleks

The next week and a half is strange. I'm working with Ben for several hours almost every day, but we're almost never alone. We're always together with equipment techs or folks from Ben's research team, so it's made for an odd working relationship. Everything we say out loud and all of our interactions are completely aboveboard and professional, but there's this undercurrent running between us. It's obvious that we're incredibly attracted to each other, and every time we venture into each other's personal space, the electricity crackles between us. I'm fucking dying to touch him, Actually, if I'm totally honest, I'm fucking dying to rip his clothes off and suck his dick, but sadly, neither of those things is happening. The odd thing is that along with his attraction, I feel a weird hostility coming from him. It makes no sense since it was he who ghosted me that first night. *I'm* the one who should be acting cold and pissed at him. But unfortunately, that's not in my nature. I've never been good at holding grudges, and the overwhelming sexual attraction I have for Ben seems to override every other emotion I have when I'm around him. Maybe it's a good thing he sometimes acts like he can't stand me because if he ever gave me an opening, I'd probably climb him like a tree. It's only when he thinks I'm not paying attention that he looks at me with open heat in his expression, and it's probably better if I don't think too much about that.

We're scheduled to attend tonight's game together. Everyone's been working hard to make sure everything is set up perfectly, so I'm feeling good about it. After tonight's game, the team will get together over the next few days to iron out any last-minute kinks in our processes for equipment care and data collection. We should be able to put the helmets into an actual live game really soon, which is exciting.

Even at the farm-team level, game days are wildly busy, and the pressure is even more intense at the NHL level. Today, I relish the million and one little things that come up in the hours leading up to game time because they work wonders at distracting me from thinking about the sexy doctor in all kinds of very unprofessional situations.

I was cold as fuck to him that first day he was in the office, and maybe that's the reason for the hostility I feel from him sometimes, but as we've spent time together over the last couple of weeks, I've been able to see what an incredible person he is. The man cares about people. Like, he really cares. He's unfailingly kind to every single person we come into contact with, from the Zamboni drivers and ice technicians at the rink, right up to Head Coach Barry Silver and Carson Wells. He brings up his stepdad in the care home fairly regularly now, and it's easy to see how much he loves his family. It makes me sad though. His dad is so young to be in a care home. I can easily understand why he chose this field of medicine to get into.

Right before the national anthem, Ben and I take our seats in the folding chairs beside the players' bench that are held aside for VIPs. I figure it's a good place to start out, and we'll move around to various locations as the game goes on. After the puck drops, I snag the two bottles of water I stashed out here for us and hand one to Ben.

"Thanks," he says gratefully, taking a long swig. I can't tear my eyes away from his Adam's apple as he swallows, and I'm mesmerized until a few seconds later when a hit takes place directly in front of us. The safety glass flexing and the *thunk* of massive bodies colliding with the wall a couple of feet from us jolt me back to reality.

"Oh, yeah, you're welcome," I stammer. "You don't notice how much running around you do on game days, but it means I don't have to bother with a workout."

When he returns my smile, my stomach flips. It's the first time I've seen his genuine smile—the one I remember from our hookup night. It makes my knees weak and sets off a flock of very excited butterflies in my stomach.

We make idle conversation during the breaks in the play until about halfway through the first period, when Carson's assistant, Kelly, appears beside my chair. It's weird to see them down here because they're normally up in the box with the other execs during games. They put their hand gently on my shoulder and lean in to whisper in my ear.

"I'm sorry to do this to you, Aleks, but Harborview Medical Center called. It's about your friend Josephine. There's an emergency, and you need to contact them. I'm sorry, I couldn't get any more info out from them because I'm not next of kin." Kelly's eyes are kind.

The blood drains out of my face as I jump to my feet, nearly knocking over my folding chair in my rush.

"What is it?" Ben asks, concern flooding his expression.

"A problem with a friend. I'll be right back," I say quickly. I push past Kelly with a muttered "thanks" over my shoulder, running as fast as my legs will carry me to the downstairs coach's office, where there's a landline, since cell phones aren't always reliable down in the bowels of the arena.

My relationship with Josie is closer than most best friends. My parents helped her become emancipated from her abusive parents when we were sixteen, something for which I will be eternally grateful. That's how Josie knows my dad so well. He helped her a lot during that horrible time. He's not a soft and fuzzy guy, but that wasn't what Josie needed back then. She needed someone to fight for her like a goddamn pit bull, and Kent Warren was perfect for that job. Even as angry as I get with my dad sometimes, deep down, I know he's a good person. My parents helped make sure Josie didn't end up in the foster system, and I firmly believe they saved her life by helping her get away from her abusive family. That means she has no biological family, so I'm always listed as her next of kin.

I clatter into the tiny office next to the locker room and dial the number on the Post-it from Kelly with shaking hands, chewing on my nails while I wait to be connected.

"Is this Mr. Aleksandr Warren?" a crisp, efficient voice asks a few moments later.

"Yes, I'm calling about Josephine Devonshire. I'm her next of kin," I say, trying to keep my voice steady.

"Yes, hello, Mr. Warren. I'm glad we tracked you down. Josephine has been asking for you. There was a car accident, and your—Josephine was injured and brought here to us. She's in surgery now for a badly broken leg, but she was able to give us your contact information before they took her in."

"Oh fuck, fuck, fuck," I whisper. "Is she... She's going to be okay, right?" I'm desperate for an answer, fearing the worst.

"None of her injuries are life-threatening, but she was badly shaken up. I'm sure she'd appreciate seeing you when she gets out of surgery." The voice is warmer now.

"Yes, yes, of course. I'll be there as soon as possible," I say, thanking all the gods that Josie isn't in danger of losing her life, but it doesn't sound good if she was asking for me. Normally, that girl is a rock, and since she knows I'm working a game tonight and was still asking for me, it means she must be scared as fuck.

I hang up the phone and go tearing out to the bench to tell people I'm leaving. I fucking hope they can handle things, but right now, I don't even care. I just need to get to Josie.

When I get to the bench, I get the attention of Dave, the Sasquatch's lead equipment manager. His eyes fill with concern when I spit out what's happening.

"Go, just go ahead, Aleks. We've got you," he says with a reassuring smile.

"Thanks, Dave. I'm so sorry. I'll contact Carson and—"

"Just go take care of your friend. I'll talk to everyone, okay? Just be safe. It's shitty weather out there," he says. I look up to the big glass window of the arena, which is at street level since this rink is built down into the ground instead of up, like most other large venues. The snow is falling so heavily it's easy to see even through the darkened windows.

"Okay, yeah, thanks," I say. I race back down the tunnel to grab my car keys and the rest of my stuff. I'm so focused I don't even notice when I run right past Ben, who's obviously standing there waiting for me.

"Wait, Aleks, what's wrong? What happened?" he asks, immediately falling into a run beside me.

"I have to go. My best friend, Josie, was in a car accident, and she's in surgery, and I'm her only family, so I have to go right now." I'm babbling as I tear into the locker room and over to the little cubby where I leave my stuff during games.

"Dave said he'll handle the equipment. Sorry, I gotta go." I push past where Ben's standing by the door, back into the tunnels that will lead me to the direct exit to the staff parking lot.

"Wait, wait," Ben calls, coming after me. "Which hospital are you going to?"

"Harborview," I say as he continues to keep pace with me.

"I'll drive you," he says with authority. "You're upset— you shouldn't drive, especially in this weather."

"It's fine, I'm fine." I push open the exit door and race toward my car. He keeps up effortlessly, like we're just out for a walk in the park.

"Aleks, stop," he finally says, grabbing my arm as we reach our cars. "I'm a doctor, and I have privileges at Harborview. I can get information faster than you, and you don't want to worry about parking. I'll drop you at the door and meet you. You'll get there faster."

I hesitate for a moment. Even though I'd rather not, I'd be stupid not to take him up on this offer. "Fine, let's go, then. Hurry," I say.

He grabs his key fob from his pocket, and the lights on his big, black Volvo SUV flash.

"Get in," he says, and within moments, we're out of the parking lot and heading through the snow-covered streets toward the hospital. It's not far, but when snow falls in Seattle, it's like something out of a horror movie. People lose access to their brains, completely forgetting any rules of the road. It's like *Mad Max* on the streets.

I have to admit, Ben's driving probably gets us there more quickly than mine would have. He lets me off at the emergency door and, after getting Jo's last name, says he'll meet me inside after he parks the car.

"Thanks," I shout as I run full speed into the emergency room, skidding to a halt in front of the check-in desk. "Hi, I got a call about my friend. She was in a car crash, and she's in surgery, and I'm her next of kin," I stammer, and the nurse gives me a kind smile, directing me down the hall to a different check-in desk, where I go through the same routine, but this time, I get checked in, and the clerk gives me a pass to clip onto my shirt, along with directions to where Josie will be when she gets out of surgery.

Once I get up to the proper waiting area, I quickly discover the meaning of "hurry up and wait." Josie is apparently still in surgery, but no one can give me any more information than what I got on the phone, so I'm stuck waiting for the doctor to come talk to me after they're done fixing her.

I'm only there a few minutes before Ben walks in, looking every inch a doctor. His presence seems to command the room, his quiet confidence sending a wave of calming energy through the space.

"What have you heard?" he asks me quietly, and after I tell him they haven't told me anything more, he goes up to the nurse's desk, where they talk in hushed tones.

He comes back a few minutes later with a bit more info. "Okay, so there isn't much more news than what you already know. There was a car accident, likely due to the bad weather. The cops didn't say anything about anyone being impaired or anything. The other driver had minor injuries and has already been released. Josephine has a badly broken leg, and they're working on it now. Most of her other injuries are bumps and bruises, nothing to be too worried about."

I nod, closing my eyes with relief. "How long will she be in surgery?"

"They aren't sure, but it shouldn't be more than another hour. The doctor will come talk with you as soon as they finish up. She's going to be okay, Aleks." He gives me a smile while reaching out to hold my shoulder, but instead of letting him comfort me like a normal person, I lunge forward, wrapping my arms around his waist and burying my face in his neck. After a moment of hesitation, he wraps his arms around me and holds me tightly against him. We stand there, not moving, for I don't know how long before he loosens his grip and leads me gently over to a row of uncomfortable plastic chairs lined up against the wall. He guides me to sit down in one, but instead of taking the seat beside me, he crouches in front of me, placing his hands on my knees, a small smile on his face. He produces one of those little packs of tissues from somewhere, so I blow my nose loudly and wipe the tears from my face, trying in vain to look a little more put together.

"I'm sorry," I say. "I didn't mean to lose it. I was just really scared."

He squeezes my knee with one of his big hands and catches my eye. "You have no reason to apologize. It's fucking scary to get a call like that. But it seems like she's going to be fine. Can I get you something to eat? After that kind of shock, you should eat something to help even out your blood sugars."

"Um, okay, but I don't want to leave in case the doctor comes out."

"That's okay, I'll go grab you something. I know where they keep all the good stuff anyway." He winks at me and pats my knee again before rising and saying a couple of words to the nurse before disappearing down the corridor.

CHAPTER 14
Ben

As I make my way down to the hospital cafeteria, I try not to let my imagination run away from me. Aleks didn't even hesitate when he got that call about his friend. He dropped everything, even though this game was really important to his career. It was clear right away that nothing is more important to him than his friend. I knew when his face went white as a sheet that something bad had happened, and I'm curious about this friend of his. According to the information the hospital has, Aleks is listed as her only next of kin—and her only contact. I can't help but wonder if they've hooked up. Maybe their relationship is closer than he's implying. He never actually said whether he was gay or somewhere else on the LGBTQIA+ rainbow. He certainly seems to be upset at the thought that she might be injured. *Not your fucking business, Jacobs. He's a free man.*

Shaking my head, I grab a few snacks and a couple of coffees from the cafeteria and bring them back to Aleks. If she's still in the OR, we're probably going to be waiting at least a couple of hours before he'll be able to see her.

I don't examine why I feel the need to stay with him. *Something to unpack another day.*

When I get back to the waiting area, Aleks is sitting in the same place I left him. He's not facedown in his phone like everyone else in the room. Instead, he's staring off into space, his red-rimmed eyes still watery. He doesn't notice me taking the seat beside him until I give him a gentle nudge.

"Oh, sorry," he murmurs. "Thanks for this," he says, giving me a grateful smile as he takes the coffee and big chocolate chip cookie. It's not exactly healthy and balanced, but there's something to be said for comfort food during times of crisis.

We sit in silence for a few minutes, sipping our coffees. Aleks nibbles on his cookie, but he doesn't make much of a dent in it.

"So how are you and Josephine friends?" I ask casually. I really am just curious—there's no ulterior motive in my question. Honest.

"Josie," he corrects with a smile. "She hates her full name. She's always planning to get it legally changed to just Josie, but it hasn't been a priority."

He lets out a deep sigh that seems to come from the deepest part of his soul before continuing. "We grew up together. Jo was one of the first kids I met when we moved here after my dad retired from hockey. I was the scrawny, super-nerdy, new kid in school. I was an easy target, and she stood up for me against a big group of bullies."

Aleks cracks a smile. "I still remember being confused when this fucking spitfire with bright red, curly hair appeared out of nowhere. She went after those fourth graders hard. I'd never seen anything quite like Josie when she was that mad, and my dad was an NHL enforcer, so it's not like I hadn't seen violence." He laughs again before his eyes become serious.

"We were besties from that day forward. She told me her parents were mean, but, hell, every kid says that sometimes, y'know?" He shakes his head and lets out a deep breath. "But I had no idea what her life was like until I was, I don't know, ten or eleven. I snuck over to her place because she hadn't been at school. I... I went to her window, and she let me in. Her mom had pushed her into something that left a huge welt on her shoulder and then smacked her around because she cried." Aleks closes his eyes, and I tighten my grip on his hand. "I didn't know parents could be like that."

He pauses and shakes his head. "Then her father came down the hall, and she pushed me into her closet to hide." He swallows, and his grip on my hand feels like a vise. "Jesus Christ, the things he said to her... I've never been able to forget the way he sounded—he was so *cold*... He was like... emotionless. Like a weird, cruel robot. My dad used to get a little scary when he got mad, but he would get hot, you know, like yelling at us and stuff. But her dad... I knew he was angry, but he was just so... detached or something. He talked to her like he was talking about the weather, in this weird, polite tone of voice, with this posh British accent, but he was saying the most horrible things. He kept telling her she was stupid and it was her fault her mom had to punish her. If she was smarter or if she behaved better, she wouldn't get in trouble so often. And then he threatened to sell her but said he probably shouldn't bother because he wouldn't get much for her anyway."

Aleks covers his eyes with his free hand and sniffles. "I was just a kid. I had no idea what to do. But after her father left the room, she begged me not to tell, and… I didn't. I let her stay in that shit for two more years. Then it got worse, and they started locking her in the basement, sometimes for a whole weekend. It was so bad. I was afraid they might do something even worse to her, so I finally told my parents, and they helped get her out. They worked with a lawyer as soon as she was old enough to be emancipated. And they made sure she got every dime of her grandmother's inheritance her parents were trying to steal from her—we found out about that later, but that's all a whole other story." He swallows hard and wipes his runny nose on the arm of his jacket like a little kid, and it almost breaks my fucking heart. Not just for his friend but for Aleks himself. Just a little kid trying to keep this horrible secret for his friend but knowing how terribly wrong it was. He picks up his coffee and stares into it. "I'll never forgive myself for not doing something when I first found out."

He looks so fucking alone I simply can't ignore my instincts screaming at me to take care of him. I release his hand and put my arm around his shoulders instead. He leans into me, and with my other hand, I take his coffee, setting it on the low table in front of us before brushing my fingers against his cheek, dashing away the few tears there. "Aleks, you were just a kid. You were there for her as much as you could be, and you did tell your parents in the end. Don't feel guilty—you did as much as any child could do. And you helped her."

He smiles wanly and takes another deep breath. "Anyway, through all that shit, Josie was always my protector. Even when she was the one who needed protection. I grew up to be a lot scrappier than the bullies counted on, but it was because Josie showed me how to be brave." His eyes fill with tears again. "Fuck, Ben, she's like my sister, way more than any of my actual siblings. If anything happened to her, I don't know... I don't know what I would do." His voice cracks as tears spill over his cheeks again. It's all

I can do not to lean in and kiss them off. Even when he's so distraught, he's fucking gorgeous.

Instead, I tuck a stray lock of his hair behind his ear and adjust us so he can lean against me more fully, with the stupid, uncomfortable plastic armrest between us. There's a clawing need inside me to make sure he's okay and, by extension, to make sure Josie is okay. He allows me to support him, and I turn my head, inhaling the citrusy scent of his shampoo. The smell takes me right back to that night we spent together, and it feels so fucking good. I sit and hold him for a while, hoping somehow some comfort can bleed out of me and into him. When I glance down at my watch, I realize there should be more information available by now. I'm about to get up to investigate when a doc walks into the room, her eyes roaming over the people inside before landing on the two of us. She must recognize me because she smiles and walks over to where we're sitting.

"Hi, is one of you Aleksandr Warren?" she asks.

"Yeah, that's me," Aleks says eagerly, jumping up. "How is she? How's Josie?"

"I'm Dr. Lola Davis. I'm an orthopedic surgeon. And Josie is going to be fine. We were able to patch up her leg pretty well, considering it wasn't in great shape when she got here. But I'm very pleased with how the surgery went, and from what I can tell right now, I'm cautiously optimistic that she won't need any follow-up surgery, although we won't know for sure until she's had some time to heal."

"Oh, thank god," Aleks breathes out, the color draining from his face again, and for a second, I worry he might actually faint, so I reach out to steady him with an arm around his waist, but he gathers himself quickly. "When can I see her?"

"She's still in recovery, but she'll probably wake up fairly soon. We'll move her to a room shortly, and then you'll be able to see her. But keep in mind she's going to be groggy and out of it for a while. After seeing her, you might want to go home to get a few hours of rest. We'll be keeping her pretty drugged up for the next few hours."

"Okay, okay, yeah, thanks. God, thank you so much, Doctor. Thank you." Aleks looks like he might cry again, so I distract the doctor by asking a little more about the severity of Josie's concussion, and she satisfies me that it's the least severe kind, which is still something to be concerned about, but much better than the alternative.

The doctor hasn't been gone ten minutes when a nurse comes back in and asks for Aleks, telling him Josie is in her room and is awake and asking for him.

"Can I bring my... um, colleague? Um, he's a doctor, so he won't do anything wrong."

The nurse and I exchange a smile.

"Aleks, I'll come with you, but I'll wait out-side, okay? She's not going to want to deal with a stranger right now. But I'll be close if you need me, okay?"

He bites his lip and nods before we follow the nurse down the hallway to a small, private corner room. She brings Aleks inside, and a few minutes later, I can hear him laughing together with a weak-er, scratchy-sounding laugh that must be Josie. A moment later, Aleks sticks his head out into the hallway, and I'm relieved to see he's smiling.

"Will you come in for a sec? She's kicking me out, but she wants to meet you first," he says.

"Um, sure, okay." I'm surprised she's interested in meeting new people, but from what Aleks said, this woman is a lot stronger than the average bear.

I recognize her instantly from the bar the night Aleks and I first met. I remember thinking she was gorgeous, but my eye was caught by Aleks, and I don't think I looked at her once after I saw him.

She has curly red hair and bright green eyes, with freckles dotted across her nose. Honestly, she looks like a real-life version of the Disney princess Merida from *Brave*.

Aleks grabs one of her hands as she waves me over to talk to her. "Dr. Jacobs, I presume," she says, cocking an eyebrow at me. Her voice sounds scratchy but strong.

"Guilty as charged," I say with a smile. "I'm glad you're okay."

"Thanks. But it'll take more than a broken leg to take me down. Anyway, I want you to take my man Aleks home, okay? You need to make sure he gets to bed. Otherwise, he will stay up and eat chocolate and ice cream all night until he has to go to work, and I know there's no way he'll call out sick. Can I trust you to take care of him?" Her tone is light and teasing, but her eyes are shooting daggers at me. Christ, if looks could kill, I'd be a fucking corpse. I'm afraid to see what she's like when she's back to full strength.

"You have my word." I smile. "I'll take him home and make sure he goes to sleep." Glancing down at my watch, I see it's not as late as I thought it was. There's still time for Aleks to get a little rest, and maybe I can talk him into calling Carson and the equipment team to say he'll be late tomorrow.

"Good," Josie says. "And no ghosting him this time, you hear me? Aleks deserves respect, and fucking sneaking out on him in the middle of the night isn't going to cut it. You do not want to get on my bad side, Dr. Jacobs." At this point, I start to worry her look may actually kill me dead right here where I stand, even in her weakened state.

"Fuck, Josie! Shut up," Aleks giggles nervously, color rising on his cheeks as he slaps her arm gently. "The man didn't do anything wrong. It's fine. It's not like we're going to hook up again anyways." He wrinkles his nose, trying to look disgusted, but I can see the smile underneath. God, he's adorable.

Josie turns her arched eyebrow to him this time. "Mmm. Yeah, sure. Okay. But I'm serious, A. Please go home to sleep. Hopefully, they'll let me out of here sometime tomorrow, and I'm going to need someone to help me, so you're gonna need to save your strength, boy. Because this girl is gonna be a handful." A shit-eating grin takes over her face, and I chuckle. Aleks rolls his eyes at her.

"What, like, are you trying to pay me back from when I had that little flu? That was no big deal!" he says, and a look of revulsion crosses her face.

"Sure, no big deal. Tell that to my living room carpet and my bathroom floor." She rolls her eyes again before waving her hands at us, shooing us out.

"Now, I need you to GTFO. This trauma survivor needs her beauty sleep." She smiles, and Aleks smacks his lips to her cheek in a gentle but sloppy kiss that causes her to squirm before he leads us out the door into the hallway.

CHAPTER 15
Aleks

Walking through the hospital, all the adrenaline that's been holding me together for the last few hours drains out of me, and I'm left feeling like a deflated balloon. We don't talk much as Ben leads me out to the hospital staff parking lot and over to his car, but I'm leaning on him pretty heavily, and by the time I climb into the passenger seat, all I want is to curl up into a ball and fall asleep. When I immediately lean back onto the headrest and close my eyes, he lets out a soft chuckle and pulls out my seat belt, reaching over my lap to buckle me in. His breath ghosts across my cheek as he leans in close to fasten it, and even in my exhausted state, my cock stirs in my pants as his warm body presses against mine just for a second. Normally, having someone do that for me would weird me right out, but I'm too exhausted to give one tiny rat's ass.

It's still snowing hard when he pulls out of the parking garage, and the drive from the area's biggest hospital to my condo is slow going, but I'm barely aware of it, unable to resist the urge to let my eyes close just for a minute. The next thing I know, Ben's standing beside me, reaching over to unbuckle my seat belt, his car parked in a luckily empty spot right across from my condo.

"Come on, sleepyhead. Let's get you inside," he whispers, his voice low and soft next to my ear.

I don't fight letting him take care of me. I just want to feel safe and have someone cuddle me and tell me it's all going to be okay. I know I shouldn't. I've already been burned by this guy once, but he seems to want to take care of me right now, and I want to let him. Handing him the keys to my apartment, I don't protest as he walks me across the quiet street, our feet making soft *shushing* sounds in the snow. We're both quiet as we make our way into the elevator and as he unlocks the door of my loft. Once we're inside, I turn to face him, blinking slowly. I can't decipher the look on his face as he sets down his keys and wallet on my hallway table and toes off his boots before turning to me and gently helping me out of my jacket, hanging it on the hook. He makes me sit down on the bench in my entryway and kneels before me, taking my shoes off gently.

"Your feetsies are all wet," he says softly with a little smile before he pulls off one of my socks, followed quickly by the other. I'm powerless to say a word as he takes care of me so sweetly. I just watch him owlishly. I don't think anyone's taken care of me this way since I was a child when I would sometimes fall asleep in the car on our way home from some evening function. I've certainly never been cared for like this by anyone I've dated. *Not that we're dating.*

Without hesitating, he scoops me up in his arms, bridal-style, and I should be embarrassed, but I'm not. All I can do is bury my head in the curve of his neck and wrap my arms around him, holding on as he carries me up to my bed. He's so warm, and he smells like cedar and man. *I don't want to let him go.*

Once we're upstairs, he puts me down beside my bed and gently slides his hands up under the sides of my Sasquatch polo shirt. I raise my arms so he can take it off, and the way his eyes darken as his pupils dilate is impossible to miss, even in my exhausted state. He bites his bottom lip as he works open the button on my pants and slides them down gently over my thighs. He kneels before me again, and I put my hands on his shoulders to steady myself as I step out of one leg and then the other until I'm standing there in just my boxer briefs. It's a weird feeling, so intimate but not sexual. I'm not even hard, even with how much he's been touching me, but there's a comfortable, warm, liquidy feeling spreading throughout my chest as he cares for me so tenderly. He stands up, and we're so close. I could just turn my face up to him, loop my arms around his neck, and pull him down into a kiss. But before I can do that, he reaches behind me to pull down the covers on my bed.

"Climb in," he says softly, his eyes locked on mine. I do what he asks, burrowing down into my soft bed. He pulls the blankets over me and sits on the edge of my bed, reaching out to caress my cheek gently, something in his eyes I can't interpret. "You need to sleep," he whispers. Suddenly, I'm gripped with fear that he's going to take off on me again.

"Don't go. Please stay. Stay with me," I whisper. I should be mortified with how I'm begging, but I've apparently abandoned any scrap of self-respect because I don't give a shit. I don't want to be alone.

There's a moment of silence before he says softly, "Of course." A moment later, he slides into bed beside me, and before I can move, he reaches out and pulls me into his broad chest. I'm so very tired, but before I let sleep drag me down into the soft blanket of unconsciousness, I turn and place a soft kiss on his pec, noting how his breath catches in his throat.

"Thank you, Ben," I whisper, and the last thing I remember is a tender kiss being placed on the top of my head and being wrapped in his strong arms, feeling completely safe and protected.

"Anything... Anything for you," he whispers, right before I sink into sleep.

Ben

Holy mother of fuck. I can't believe I'm in Aleks Warren's bed. Again. He was utterly drained after we left Josie at the hospital. Knowing she's going to be fine allowed him to start processing all the emotions of the evening he'd been holding back, and it's a lot. It sounds like the bond between Josie and Aleks is incredibly special. Thinking about Josie's story breaks my heart, not only for little Josie, suffering at the hands of abusive parents, but for little Aleks, being so young and not knowing how to handle something so heavy. No child should ever have to learn how cruel the world is at such a young age.

The fact that Aleks dropped everything to run to his friend without a second thought is giving me pause. It doesn't fit with the mental picture I've constructed of him. One where he's a calculating, heartless individual who's far more concerned with his own best interests than anyone else. But he could not have cared less about his job when the hospital called him. On top of that, what he told me about how his parents helped

Josie is messing with the image I have of his father. The Kent Warren who lives in my head is just this side of a monster, but the person who did everything in his power to help a friend of his young son doesn't jibe with that picture.

I don't know what's going to happen in the morning when we wake up. I don't know what any of this means. I've been telling myself over and over that Aleks Warren can never be anything more to me than a coworker. But I couldn't help the urge I felt to take care of him when he needed someone. And clearly, wherever our relationship stands currently, it's more than simply coworkers. I don't think that particular job description contains anything about snuggling into bed with him, holding him tightly, and placing soft, gentle kisses to his forehead while he sleeps.

The problem is, I can't get past the fact that his father's actions caused a huge amount of harm to my family. How on earth could I even think about bringing Aleks home to them? But maybe I'm crazy to even be worrying about it at all. Maybe I need to stop overthinking this whole thing and let it happen. Take things as they come. It's not like I'm great at relationships. The chances of us ever getting to the point where I would want to bring him to meet my family are fairly slim, as depressing as that sounds. Fuck, I don't know. But right now, his warm body curled up against mine feels all kinds of right, so, just for a little while, I'm going to let myself experience this. He needed someone to take care of him, and I was happy to do it. I'm going to do my best not to borrow trouble.

That, of course, is easier than it sounds, and it takes me a long time to fall asleep. Eventually, I'm able to drift off, and the warm, snuggly body pressed into me just feels so good it's hard to imagine how I'm ever going to sleep without it.

CHAPTER 16
Aleks

B linking awake, it takes me a minute to figure out that I'm in my own bed and a second longer to realize I'm not alone. The soft, warm pillow I'm cozied up to is actually a person, and that person is none other than my current coworker, Dr. Benjamin Jacobs.

A hot second later, it all comes back to me: getting the call about Josie's accident, Ben driving me to the hospital, waiting with me for Jo to be done in surgery, and then driving me home. I don't remember much after getting home; I must have been so exhausted, combined with the letdown from the adrenaline, I was probably no better than if I was totally wasted.

I can tell the exact second Ben regains consciousness because he stiffens against me, and unfortunately, it's not in the good way. I tilt my head up so I can see his face, but I deliberately leave my lower half pressed against his side. I'm not going to let him make this weird. No matter what ends up happening between us, I'm incredibly grateful for what he did for me last night, and I want him to know.

"Good morning," I murmur. God, he's so cute in the morning. His dark hair is mussed up, and without his glasses, he looks younger than usual. He blinks at me as if he's getting his bearings before a tentative smile crosses his face.

"Morning," he says, his voice rough with sleep. "How are you feeling this morning? You were pretty drained last night."

God, he's so sweet. Where did he even come from? "I'm actually good," I say. Taking a chance, I rub my hand across the warm skin of his chest, and I'm pleased to feel the shiver that rolls through his body. "Yesterday was a lot. Thank you so much for being there for me, Ben."

He bites his bottom lip. "It was nothing," he says. "Anyone would have done the same. You were really concerned about your friend."

I shake my head. Even in the short amount of time we've spent together, I know he has a habit of brushing off and denying compliments. "Nope. Not every-one would have done the same. You were incredible, Ben. Really. You made it so much easier for me to cope with my stress over Josie. Thank you." I grab his chin between my thumb and forefinger, moving his head so he has to meet my eyes. A blush rises in his cheeks, but he holds my gaze, a tiny little smile threatening to curl up the edges of his lips.

"Okay. Well, you're welcome. I... I'm glad you let me help you." He clears his throat and moves under me, shifting his gaze so he's no longer meeting my eyes. "I'm... I really am sorry about the way I left you that first night, Aleks. I shouldn't have left like that. I just... panicked, I guess?"

I really want to ask what the hell happened to make him take off in a panic, but before I can, he changes the subject. "Josie is lucky to have you as a friend, you know. I really admire you for putting her above everything else when she needed you."

That seems like a weird thing to say. I cock my head to the side, giving him a confused look. "Well, of course. I mean, she was hurt. Wouldn't anyone do the same for their best friend?"

Ben stares at me for a minute, something I can't interpret happening behind his brown eyes. "You'd be surprised," he says after a moment. "Not everyone takes as good care of their friends. A lot of people put themselves first."

"Well, that's not me," I say, unable to figure out if he's getting at something deeper or if he's just had bad experiences with friends or something. "My friends are really important to me. Especially Jo."

He nods and tightens his arms around me. "I can tell. And that's just... really... admirable." He gives me a tentative smile.

I don't tell him that part of the reason I value my friendships so much is because I spent a lot of years watching my dad. He played hockey for so many years, in a game that's supposedly known for the strong relationships between players. But he barely kept in touch with anyone. Sure, he knows tons of people, and my parents entertain a lot, but few would be considered real friends. Most are just acquaintances. It makes me a little sad when I think about it, but I'm well aware of where my father's priorities lie.

We lie in comfortable silence for a few minutes. I don't want to admit to myself how amazing it feels to lie here in his arms. It's like we've managed to create this cozy little bubble around us, and as much as I'd like to stay in it, my head is already filling up with all the things I need to do as soon as possible. I can tell Ben's got a lot on his mind as well, but even though we're both in our heads, it's nice being together. It's comfortable in a way I wouldn't have expected. Something about Ben gives me this sense that no matter what, everything is going to be okay. I could get used to that.

"So, um, I need to check in on Josie and then contact the team and stuff, but can I interest you in one of my world-famous breakfast burritos after that?" I say, hoping my voice doesn't betray how very much I want him to say yes. I like having him in my space.

"Um. Yeah, sure, that sounds great," he says as a pleased little smile curls up the corners of his mouth, like maybe he was hoping I'd ask him to stay.

"Good," I reply, and I lean in, giving him a little peck on the cheek before reaching over to my nightstand to grab my phone. There are several text messages, but the first one I check is from Josie.

> Jo: Hey Babe. I'm awake, feel like dog vomit. Docs say everything is okay, but they want to keep me here one more night. Probably let me out tomorrow.

Instead of texting her back, I call, and she picks up immediately.

"Hey, love," she says, her voice sounding a little weak. "Before you say anything, thank you so much for coming last night. I don't even remember asking for you, but I was pretty out of it when they brought me in. I don't know what I'd do without you, boo." Her voice cracks on the last word, and I have to swallow down the lump in my throat. I'm not able to contemplate what would happen if I ever lost Josie.

"Oh, Jo, I'm glad they called me. I love you, crazy girl, but you scared the shit out of me. You are never allowed to do that again."

She gives a raspy chuckle. "I love you too, silly boy." I know she's trying to keep it light, but there's an unusual tremor in her voice. "I promise, I really will try not to scare you like that again. It wasn't as much fun as you might think."

"Good," I say. "I'm going to come by later to hang out with you, and we can make some plans for organizing help for when you get home. I can stay at your place with you for a few days at least, but we should get Tara to come too, and—" My mind is spinning with all the things I'm going to need to set up so she has all the help she needs while her leg is out of commission. She's going to hate it.

"Wait, hold up, hon," she interrupts. "I'm going to let you do all that for me, I promise. I know I have no choice. But today, I just want some time alone, okay? I need time to digest... everything. Does that make sense?"

I'm reluctant to leave her alone all day, but I know how much of an introvert Josie is. Being in the hospital is probably driving her insane with all the activity and people fussing over her. "Okay," I say hesitantly. "I will agree to leave you alone today as long as you promise to call me if you need anything at all, okay? And you also have to promise to let me be there when you're allowed to go home so I can hear all the instructions for taking care of you.

"Yeah, okay," she agrees after a moment's hesitation, and I allow myself a little smile of victory because getting my best friend to accept help is always a big win.

While I was talking with Josie, Ben slipped out of bed and disappeared downstairs with his own phone. But I like being near him, so before I read any more of my waiting messages, I slip on a pair of track pants and pad downstairs, where I find him sitting on my couch, the coffee maker perking away happily on the counter. I really like the way this little scene looks. Ben Jacobs feels like he fits into my space. And I like it a lot.

"Hey," he says with a soft smile as I plop down beside him. His eyes light up when he sees me, and my heart flutters in my chest. "How's Josie feeling?"

"She seems okay," I say. "Not herself though. And she asked me not to visit today. She says she needs time alone to process things."

Ben's eyebrows furrow with concern. "Do you think she's okay? Should she talk to someone?" My heart flutters once again as I see the genuine way he cares for my friend.

"I think she'll be okay," I say. "It's not unusual for her to want to be alone to process heavy things. And I think if she needs to talk to someone, she will. I'll make her if I have to, but she's pretty good about taking care of herself that way.

Ben nods, seemingly satisfied with that answer. "Did you get a message from Carson?" he asks.

I raise my eyebrows. "Um, no, I haven't checked that yet. Shit, is he pissed about me leaving last night?" Fuck, that'll be the last thing I need.

"No, no, not at all," he says. "Check your messages, but he wants both of us to take a few days off and get a fresh start on everything after they get back from their California road trip. They'll be back Sunday night after their game in San Francisco. He suggested we start fresh on Monday morning with getting all their equipment techs onboarded."

I scroll down to the text from Carson's assistant, Kelly. Sure enough, they relay the same message, expressing concern for me and my friend and asking me to let them know if the team can provide any kind of help or support. They even attached a list of support services, which all team staff have access to, including home health care services for family members. Kelly even added a note at the bottom, letting me know that I do qualify for these services now that I'm part of the Sasquatch staff.

"Wow," I say, a little shocked by the team's generosity. I know most pro teams take really good care of their people, but usually, the best perks are reserved for players. And I've barely even started my job with the team. I can't believe they're giving me all these benefits so soon. "God, they're really stepping up. It's incredible." I tell Ben about all the things the team offered to do to help me and, by extension, Josie.

"That's great news. They seem like a good organization. Carson Wells seems like a different kind of manager, but he sure seems to have his priorities straight," Ben says.

"Yeah," I agree. "These services will help Jo a lot, and not having to search around to find people to take care of her takes a lot of weight off my shoulders."

Ben smiles at me again, his eyes searching mine, for what, I don't know. "Yeah. That's what all businesses should do though, right? Take care of their people? And you and Josie both deserve it, Aleks. You're an amazing friend to her. She's really lucky to have you."

God, I wish I could figure out what's going on in his head. He looks so serious when he talks about friendship and how impressed he is that I'm being a good friend to Josie. But it confuses me. I kind of thought that's what friendships are supposed to be. I guess maybe Ben's experiences haven't been that way.

"Um, anyway," I say. "It seems like we both have a couple of days off. Do, um, do you have any plans? Because I was thinking if you don't, maybe we could hang out? Maybe do some fun Christmassy stuff or something?" I'm not sure where that came from, but it's out of my mouth anyway. It definitely feels like I'm asking him for a date. And I guess maybe I am. Things have changed between us over the last day. I know I'm seeing him differently, and I hope he's seeing me as more than just a hookup.

He looks at me for a moment, blinking. But then a smile crosses his face, and fucking hell, he's so gorgeous.

"Yeah. That would be great. Let's do that," he says, and a big flock of butterflies launches in my tummy. I have no idea what I'm doing here, and it's very possible this man will just break my damn heart. But the more time I spend with him, the more convinced I am that I need to shoot my shot. I'll have to worry about picking up the pieces later.

CHAPTER 17
Ben

I don't know what I'm doing. I shouldn't be hanging out with Aleks. We're just coworkers. There's no future for us anywhere. But the problem is, I really, really like being around him. He's not who I thought he was. He's so far away from the entitled little shit I would have expected Kent Warren's son to be it makes me shake my head. He was genuinely thrilled when he saw that the team was going to give him access to all the medical and caretaker benefits, even though he only just started, and technically, he isn't even certain his job with the Sasquatch is permanent. Of course, I may have texted Carson with an update on the situation while Aleks was talking with Josie earlier. I didn't exactly ask for Aleks to have access to all the benefits I know team employees get, but I may have implied that it would be helpful. Carson acted on it right away, which impresses me.

After making plans to do some Christmas-type activities together, I head back to my place to grab a change of clothes and shower. Without spending a lot of time overthinking it, I throw a couple of days' worth of clothing into a bag, along with my toothbrush. Never hurts to be prepared.

My palms are sweaty as I ring the buzzer when I get back to his place. It's ridiculous—I don't know why I'm nervous. I slept in his bed last night, for god's sake. And not long ago, we did a lot more than just sleep in his bed. So, I shouldn't have anything to be so nervous about. But here I am.

He answers the buzzer, saying he'll be right down, and when he appears, I swallow hard and wipe those sweaty palms on my jeans because he looks good enough to eat. He's wearing dark jeans and a camel-colored Filson jacket over a red sweater, which brings out his bright green eyes. A red-and-black buffalo plaid scarf wrapped around his neck completes his outfit, and his smile makes me want to melt, even though it's freezing out here.

"Hey," I say as soon as he opens the door, trying to sound casual but failing miserably. "You ready?"

Smooth. Asking if he's ready when you're already walk-
ing out the door. Good job, Jacobs.

Aleks grins. "Sure am. Let's go."

He says he wants to go pick up some things for Josie's house to help make things a little easier for her when she comes home, so we head to Target to grab a few practical household items before heading downtown to shop for some fun gifts for her.

Westlake Center in downtown Seattle is the main shopping hub. It's stopped snowing, finally, but there are several inches of the white stuff on the ground, but even with the weather, the area is busy, and the giant Christmas tree in Westlake Center towers over the busy shoppers. I don't know what possesses me to do it, but I reach out and grab Aleks' hand as we're walking around. He startles at first, and he looks down at our clasped hands. A smile crosses his face, and when his eyes meet mine, he looks so gorgeous I lose my breath. His bright green eyes behind his glasses, his rosy cheeks and red lips. I want to kiss him so badly I'm almost shaking, but instead, I just reach out and adjust his scarf, taking the opportunity to let my fingertips brush against his neck. His quick intake of breath makes my cock jump in my jeans, and I have to bite my lip to stop the groan from escaping.

After he finds a few fun things for Josie, including some extra cozy pj's made from super-stretchy material that should fit over her cast, we head back to my car. At one point, the thought crosses my mind that it might be fun to pick out a Christmas tree together, but it seems like such a couple-y thing to do I don't suggest it right away. But Aleks is so genuinely delighted over all the Christmas decorations and the gifts he picks out it makes my chest feel tight and weird. But instead of worrying that I might be having some kind of heart attack, I decide to just say, fuck it, and plunge headfirst into... whatever this is...

"So, um, how would you feel about maybe going to get a Christmas tree?" I ask hesitantly, but my nerves disappear when his face lights up like the proverbial Christmas tree.

"Oh my god, are you serious? I would love that!"

I laugh because, fuck me sideways, he's seriously adorable.

"I was thinking we could go cut our own, but considering the time and the roads, maybe we could go to this awesome lot over in Woodinville where they have really good precut ones. What do you think?" I ask.

Aleks giggles with delight, the sound making my heart do a weird flutter in my chest. "Well, I'm a bit of a purist when it comes to cutting down my own Christmas tree, but maybe this time, we can make an exception. Let's do it!"

I bark out another laugh, catching his enthusiasm. "Let's see what we can find."

The drive to the tree farm in Woodinville, northeast of Seattle, isn't long, even with the messy roads, and before long, we're pulling into the small, thankfully plowed parking lot. A little red barn with white trim sits beside the parking area; to one side of it is the large field where the U-cut trees grow, and the lot containing their precut selection on the other. Despite the weather, there are several families with young kids bundled up and making their way either out into the field of trees, saws in hand, or on their way back, with the lot employees helping them get the lucky trees loaded into their vehicles for the ride home.

"Alright, then, let's find you the perfect tree," I say as we get out of the car.

Aleks giggles again and grabs onto my arm as we head across the lot, and we each grab a red Solo cup of the hot apple cider they're handing out at the entrance. The rows of evergreen trees stand proudly, and their sharp, clean scent fills the air, mingling with the sweet cinnamon scent of our cider.

"Wait a second," he says, "what about a tree for you?"

"Well, honestly, I don't usually put one up anymore," I say a little sheepishly. "I always celebrate at my mom's house or at my stepdad's care home when I'm not working over Christmas anyway."

"Oh no, Dr. Jacobs, that simply will not do!" His voice is teasing. "You mean to tell me you don't even put up your own Christmas tree, yet you're capable of finding the so-called 'perfect tree'?" He makes air quotes.

"Well, I do have some expertise in the area," I say seriously. "I worked at a tree lot for a couple of seasons while I was in high school."

"Nice! So you are actually a true expert. I'm impressed," he says, his eyes sparkling. "So, tell me, Ben, what, in your expert opinion, makes a tree perfect?" he asks. "Would it be the height? Shape? Proper number of branches to ensure optimal ornament distribution? I need all your secrets, come on." He gives me a pleading look, batting his lashes coquettishly.

"Well," I reply, tapping my chin thoughtfully, "those factors are all important, but the biggest thing is the tree's personality. It has to have that certain... *je ne sais quoi.*"

"Wooow." He widens his eyes and pretends to rest his chin on the back of his hands like he's enraptured by my thoughts on tree selection. "Please tell me more, oh Master Tree Whisperer."

"Hey, I take my tree selection seriously," I defend, loving the way he's still hanging on to my arm as we amble through the tree lot.

He nods seriously. "I can see that." A moment later, he leans over to take a close look at a tree we're passing. "Look at this one. It's got the scent of a winner about it, don't you think?" he asks.

I stop, taking a long look at the tree he's standing beside. "I can see the potential, certainly, but we can't choose the first good one we see. Let's keep it in mind and circle back after we check out the rest. I mean, checking out the entire selection is a critical part of the process."

"Oh, of course, that makes sense," he laughs as we continue wandering through the rows of spruce and fir trees. In this moment, everything feels light and easy, as if the weight of everything that's gone between us before has been lifted. Aleks is like sunshine in a bottle. It's addictive, but I need to be careful. He would be easy to fall for. Too easy. And I can't let that happen.

A few minutes later, he pauses, looking intently at a medium-sized fir. "What do you think of this one?" he asks, and I step closer to him, pulling it out and lifting it a bit so we can get a closer look, checking its branches and needles.

"Wow, you weren't kidding. You do take this seriously, don't you?" His grin is huge and so sweet. He looks like the sweetest little Christmas elf, all bundled up in his red scarf. *Fuck, I want to kiss him so bad.*

"So what's the verdict?"

I take a step back, nodding slowly, appraising the candidate. "Well, it's got a nice symmetrical shape. No obviously dead or dying needles. Overall feel is good, a combination of elegance and comfort." I bite down on my lip, making a show of thinking hard. "Yes, this is it. I decree this tree worthy of your apartment."

Aleks bursts out laughing. "Awesome. Let's do it."

We have one of the lot kids wrap up our chosen winner and help us put it in the back of my SUV, and fifteen minutes later, we're getting back in the car, and I'm cranking the heat to warm up our cold toes and fingers. We share another laugh when both our glasses fog up at the sudden change in temperature, but a few minutes later, we're on our way. The sun is already sliding toward the horizon when we head back across Lake Washington to Seattle proper.

"So, can I interest you in dinner?" I ask. I know I shouldn't, but god, I just like him. I mean, sure, I want to fuck him again, but I also really like spending time with him. He shoots me some side-eye from the passenger seat as he chews on his lip. I can't tell if he's trying to let me down easy or if he's debating with himself as to whether continuing this "date that's not a date" is wise. Part of me wants to backpedal and find a way to take back the offer, but a much bigger part of me is simply hoping he says yes.

"Yeah, I'd like that," he finally says.

I don't think either one of us really gets what's going on between us. There are so many reasons continuing this "date" is a bad idea, but honestly, fuck it. It's just dinner. It's not like we're getting married.

We end up at a small, out-of-the way restaurant not too far from Aleks' place that I've never visited but have heard good things about. Since it's still early, we get a table right away. The soft murmur of conversation and the faint hum of holiday tunes in the background create a cozy atmosphere.

We each order a glass of wine, and I take a moment to appreciate how gorgeous Aleks is as the soft lighting from the votive candles on the tables bathes us in a comfortable glow.

He looks at me, holding the stem of the wineglass between his thumb and forefinger, stroking it up and down thoughtfully. The unintentionally suggestive movement causes my cock to jump in my pants. *Stand down, soldier.*

Aleks licks his lips, and I have to bite back a groan. God, I want him again. No more denying it.

"Today was really fun. Thank you," he says almost shyly. "And thanks again for helping me last night. If you hadn't been there, it would have been so much harder."

"It was nothing, no trouble at all," I say, reflexively brushing off his gratitude.

He arches an eyebrow. "It *really* was *not* nothing. You took off from the game to help me, drove me there in the snow, you stayed with me all that time, and then you even drove me home. It was something, Ben, not nothing. It was a lot, and I'm really grateful."

Our eyes lock, and I swallow, nodding. "Okay. You're welcome. I was happy to help."

The air is charged, electricity crackling between us. A smile plays around the corners of his mouth as he takes a sip from his wineglass, and it's killing me not to lean in and kiss him. There's something special about Aleks Warren. I'm drawn to him like I've never been drawn to another person.

The spell around us breaks when the server returns to take our order, but after he disappears, the sexual tension may have decreased, but it's not gone. Not by a long shot.

"Okay, so, tell me, Dr. Jacobs, I'm curious: have you ever regifted?"

I bark out a laugh at the non sequitur. He has a way of constantly surprising me. I let out an exaggerated gasp, clutching my chest. "Never!" I say with a shocked expression. "Have you?"

He grins wickedly. "Wouldn't you like to know?" We both laugh before he continues. "Fine, I admit it. Maybe once or twice, but only for really shitty gifts."

"Like a label maker?" I laugh, not expecting him to pick up on my slightly obscure *Seinfeld* reference. But he snorts a laugh, getting it right away.

"Exactly! I didn't blame Tim Whatley one bit! If someone gives me a label maker, you can bet it's getting regifted, *tout de suite*."

"Favorite Christmas movie?" I ask.

"*Elf*. Hands down," he says. "Yours?"

"*Christmas Vacation*, one hundred percent," I laugh. "Nothing better than Cousin Eddie emptying the RV toilet into the storm sewer. 'Shitter was full!'"

We share another laugh. "We should totally have a Christmas movie marathon," Aleks blurts out, and then he freezes, his eyes widening like he didn't mean for that to come out of his mouth. "Um, I didn't mean, like, together or anything, I know you're not—"

"I'd love that. Let's do it." I say, and his eyes widen again.

"Yeah, really? You'd want to?"

"Yeah. I really would."

The conversation flows effortlessly as we continue eating, punctuated by laughter and teasing. By the time dessert arrives, we've each moved in our chairs so our legs are intertwined under the table, his foot resting between mine. I'm extremely aware of where our bodies are pressed together, even though there are layers of clothing between us. My mind drifts back to how good he feels when there's nothing separating us. Hot skin pressed against hot skin. My cock hardens in my jeans, and I have to shift to avoid getting a zipper imprint embedded on it.

Of course, Aleks notices, and he shoots me a cheeky grin, but I'm saved by the server returning to ask if we need anything else.

"No, thank you. I think we're ready to go, actually," I say.

After taking care of the bill, we head back to Aleks' loft, where we make short work of pulling the tree out of my car and carrying it up to his loft, where we quickly unwrap it. Magically, Aleks produces a tree stand from who knows where, so we get it set up and then stand back to admire it.

"I think it's perfect, don't you? Aleks asks. "Even undecorated, it's perfect. I can't wait to bust out my decorations. Hey, maybe you can help me with that tomorrow. Josie and I usually do it together, but she's not going to be much help, obviously. She could supervise from the couch while we hang the decorations. Then I could make us something yummy for dinner. I know she's going to need to eat—" He freezes again, looking embarrassed. "Um, I mean, if you don't have other plans. If you want to, that is. I didn't mean to assum—"

The rest of his sentence is unintelligible because I finally hit my breaking point. Closing the distance between us, I grab his face between my hands and crush my mouth onto his.

CHAPTER 18
Aleks

Fucking finally. Ben's mouth lands on mine like he's been starving for me, and if he feels anything like I do right now, he has. He walks us backward until I'm pressed against the wall, and I lean into it, pulling him into me. His bigger body pressing against mine with the hard wall behind me feels fucking exquisite, and a growly noise escapes from the very bottom of my lungs. "Holy fuck," I gasp when he makes his way along my jaw, licking and tasting at my skin like I'm his favorite Christmas treat. He pulls back, and my breath catches when he presses two fingers against my lips, which are puffy from our rough kisses. I suck them into my mouth, loving the groan that escapes him when I suck hard and swirl my tongue around them like I'm giving him a blowjob.

His hips jerk, his cock like an iron rod against me. Releasing his fingers from my mouth with a pop, we hold each other's gaze for a moment, both of us flushed and panting, our chests rising and falling against each other.

"Fuck, I've been waiting to do that again since that first night," he rasps, the urgency in his voice causing molten heat to gather in the pit of my belly.

"Me too," I say breathlessly. "Upstairs, now," I growl.

He grabs my hand, and we race up the stairs to my bed, where I push him back onto it before making short work of his jeans and yanking them roughly down his thighs. He wrestles off his own shirt at the same time as I slide my fingertips under the waistband of his briefs, pulling them down enough that his dick pops out. I almost drool as I take in his thick cock standing at attention for me.

I strip out of my own clothes quickly, my eyes never leaving Ben's as he rips his jeans and underwear the rest of the way off, then lies back against the pillows, stroking himself, his pupils blown out and his chest still rising and falling rapidly. The naked desire on his face makes me feel powerful as I climb over him, rising onto my knees and palming my own cock, staring down at him.

"You wanna suck my cock?" My voice sounds deep and rough. His eyes widen, and he stares at my hand moving up and down my shaft. Leaning back so he can get a good look, I rub my thumb over my slit to gather the bead of precome gathered there before bringing it to my lips, letting out another groan as I taste myself. His mouth drops open like he's surprised. He's not the only one—I'm not usually this bold in bed. But something about Ben gives me confidence. I feel safe with him, and it's like I'm invincible. I can let go of everything and do whatever I want, or ask for whatever I want. It's a fucking heady feeling, and I don't want to lose it.

He growls and grabs my erection, squeezing me hard.

"Yeah, I want to suck your gorgeous cock," he says. "I love your dick. Wanna feel it in my mouth."

I shuffle forward so I'm straddling his chest, and he grabs my thighs as I guide my cockhead to his lips, pausing for a moment to trace them with my tip, watching in fascination as they glisten with my precome.

Ben huffs out a breath, and I shiver as it ghosts across the sensitive head of my erection, and then he breathes in deeply, inhaling my scent. "Goddamn, you smell so fucking hot. Give it to me, Aleks. I need to suck your hot cock."

Oh, sweet Jesus on ice skates. That's the hottest thing anyone's ever said to me.

Ben sticks his tongue out and drags it over my crown, and I nearly combust right there. The hot, wet feel is like nirvana.

I have to lean forward to brace myself on the headboard, otherwise my shaking legs will never hold me up, and from this angle, I watch as he licks up and down my dick like it's a lollipop. One of his hands holds it at the base, and the other one is wrapped around my thigh. Without warning, he pulls me forward so he envelops me completely in his hot mouth, and I moan loudly. The pleasure shoots through me like an electric current running from my cock right down to my toes.

"You like sucking my big dick," I hiss, and he groans, nodding. Seeing his mouth stretched around me feels like my own personal porn. He tilts his head back so he can meet my eyes, and his are wild as he increases the intensity of his sucking. A moan tears from me, and I feel like a fucking beast as I thrust into him.

He pops off me for a second to whisper harshly, "Fuck my face, Aleks. Go hard. I want it." Then he swallows me down again, taking me so deep I hit the back of his throat, causing him to gag. He works through it and keeps sucking me like a fucking champ until I give in, fucking his face like he asked, plunging into his hot, wet heat over and over again. The orgasm starts pooling at the base of my spine, and I spread my knees an inch wider, sinking even further into his throat. He moans approvingly while rubbing and pulling at my balls, running his fingers through the saliva coating my skin. Then he drags his hand back, still sucking me deep while his fingers play with my hole, using his spit like lube as he circles my rim.

I whimper. "Oh Jesus, yes, Ben, fuck me with your fingers while I fuck your mouth. Yes, oh fuck, do it. Put them in."

He shakes underneath me, and we groan together as he pushes a finger into me. I bite my cheek and slap my hand against the wall to keep from screaming in pleasure.

The sensations swamping me have turned the world upside down. I don't know whether to push my cock into his hot mouth, or my ass back onto his slick finger. He plunges another digit into my hole, and I'm so close. His mouth is on my cock, the fingers of one hand deep inside my ass as he starts jerking himself with his other hand.

"Oh, god, yes, Ben, jerk yourself off while you fuck my ass with your fingers and swallow my cock. Yes, oh fuck, yes, yes..."

His deep groans and the sound of his hand shuttling up and down his cock push me over. Every muscle tenses and my orgasm slams into me like an F5 tornado as I unload into his mouth, pumping stream after stream of come deep into his throat. He makes a gurgling sound of appreciation as I flood his mouth before his own storm hits, his back arching off the mattress and his eyes squeezed shut as he coats the backs of my thighs with warm come.

"Oh my god," I whisper harshly as I pull out of his mouth and fall to the bed beside him. "That was fucking amazing."

He throws an arm over his eyes, still breathing hard. "Fuck yeah it was," he pants.

Ben

"Jesus Christ, I think you might have killed me," I chuckle after lying quietly together for a few minutes. I turn my head to find him grinning at me.

"But what a way to go," he quips.

I nod, still chuckling. "At least you can say I died doing what I loved." We both snicker.

"One second," he murmurs before rolling out of the bed and returning a second later to clean me up with a warm towel. Normally I prefer to be the caretaker, but with Aleks, it feels like there's a more natural give-and-take. Those instincts are still there, but part of me wants to let go and let him be in charge some-times, which is weird. Letting myself be taken care of isn't something I usually do, but it feels nice. It occurs to me that I might want something from Aleks that I haven't wanted from a partner in a long time. I'm normally a top. Bottoming makes me feel vulnerable, and I'm not willing to go there with someone unless I've already built up a lot of trust with them. But right from the start, Aleks has made me feel unusually comfortable.

He tosses the towel onto the floor and crawls back into bed beside me, resting his head on my chest. I like the way it feels so much I wrap one arm around his back to anchor him there, trying not to notice the way my heart flips in my chest when he lets out a content sigh.

I clear my throat. *In for a penny, in for a pound, I guess.* "So, ah, do you ever top?" I ask, trying to swallow my discomfort at the question. But even the fact that I'm asking says a lot about my feelings toward this man.

He lifts his head from where it's resting on my chest and gives me a look that pulls a laugh from me. He looks like a kid who's just been given the exact Christmas gift he's been asking Santa for. His eyes are as bright as Christmas lights, and his face looks like it might split in two from the grin on it.

"Do I ever top? Mmm. Yes, yes, I can definitely be persuaded to top." He chuckles, and my eyes widen.

"Are you... Is that what you prefer?" I ask, worried that I've somehow pushed him into bottoming when that's not what he actually wants. He laughs again, patting my chest reassuringly.

"I'm just teasing you. I'm vers, but I tend to prefer bottoming. Although, topping the right person is... enjoyable. And you? Are you an exclusive top?"

I shake my head. "I would call myself vers too, although I prefer topping. I find bottoming to be a little more... intimate... so I don't want that from everyone."

Aleks pauses for a moment, his gaze shifting down to where he's running his fingers through my chest hair before he looks back up at me. "And, you... You'd want that from me?"

I nod. "Yeah. I think I do." *Gah, what is it about Aleks Warren? Why am I so comfortable sharing all my fucking secrets with him?*

He looks at me for a moment, something shining in his eyes I can't identify, before he shifts so his body is on top of mine, and he looks down at me. "I want that too, Ben. I really fucking want that."

He takes my mouth in a tender kiss that's anything but tentative. He's sweet but confident. Like he knows exactly what he wants, and he's perfectly confident in showing me.

We break apart briefly, and he reaches over to his nightstand, grabbing a couple of condoms and a bottle of lube, setting them on the bed beside us while he shimmies backward and settles between my legs. Once he's there, he looks up at me with a smile, looking like that same kid who just got a toy from Santa he's been waiting for all year. "Oh, I'm gonna enjoy this," he whispers before taking just the crown of my dick into his mouth and sucking gently but firmly.

"Unngggh," I groan, my dick going from semi-hard to an iron rod almost instantly. "Fuck, you really are gonna kill me. I'm not twenty-four anymore, you know?"

He laughs again. "Well, as I said before, at least you'd get to go doing what you love," he jokes before sucking me entirely into his hot, wet mouth, taking me right to the back of his throat.

Pleasure courses through me as he sucks, and I throw my head back, enjoying the sensations until I hear the *snick* of the lube bottle opening. Opening my eyes, I see him slicking up his fingers before he moves one hand between my legs and pushes one against my entrance.

"Is this okay?" he breathes out as that finger circles my rim, pressing and pulling back, teasing me just enough to drive me crazy with want.

"So much better than okay." I gasp as he takes my cock into his mouth again at the same time as he presses his fingertip inside me, tearing a loud moan from my chest.

"Oh fuuuuck." I push down on his finger, willing my body to open up and let him inside.

Slowly, he works his fingers in deeper, coaxing my body open, and it's so good it's like he's stealing the breath from my lungs.

I'm suddenly overcome by the need to see him. To watch what he's doing to me. With effort, I raise myself onto my elbows, looking down my body at him, his head bent over as he sucks my impossibly hard dick into his mouth. With one hand, he caresses my abs, and the other hand pumps his finger gently in and out of my body. He shifts so we can make eye contact, his mouth stretched wide around my dick, and I feel like my soul leaves my goddamn body as he slides another finger inside me, crooking them both and grazing that bundle of nerves that makes me see fireworks.

"Unnngh... Fuck, Aleks, I need you. Need you inside me now." I collapse back, squeezing my eyes shut as I try desperately not to explode in his mouth. I want to feel him inside me. Fuck, I want to feel everything with him. *Everything.*

Releasing my dick from his mouth, he places hot, open-mouthed kisses from my groin to my hip bone. "You're ready? You're sure?" he asks, gently scissoring his fingers in a stretch that burns for a few moments before dissolving into overwhelming pleasure.

The noise that comes out of me sounds like some kind of animal in distress, and in my desperation, that's what I feel like. About to lose my ever-loving mind with pleasure, I'm afraid I might literally die if he doesn't fuck me right now.

"Aleks, please.. please..." I beg. I'm not even embarrassed about it.

"Okay, okay, baby, it's alright. I'll take care of you, don't worry," he soothes, and even though I'm so desperate, something settles inside me. He's so sincere and so fucking sweet. I watch him as he quickly rolls the condom over his hard dick, and I breathe a sigh of relief as he notches his cockhead against my entrance.

For a minute, vulnerability surges through me. It's been a while since I allowed myself to feel this with another person, but our eyes lock, and the only thing I see is someone who wants to make me feel good. Someone who cares enough to take care of me. I take a deep breath, willing myself to relax, and as he pushes forward into me, I reach out and touch his cheek with my hand. He wraps a hand around my dick and strokes me with a firm grip, sliding his hand upward, making me shudder at the pleasure.

Inch by inch, he slides into me, slowly enough that I can adjust to the intrusion, and I keep taking deep breaths, willing my body to open up all the way and allow him inside me as deep as he can go. I slide my knees up higher, breathing rhythmically in and out as he bottoms out inside me. A shiver rolls through his whole body, and a sense of pride fills me, knowing he's affected by this connection we have, the same as me.

He stops, his hips pressed tightly against my ass. His eyes search mine. "You okay?" he whispers.

"Yeah," I say softly, my eyes on his, my hand caressing his cheek. God, he's beautiful.

"God, you feel so good. *So... good...*" he whispers.

I move my hands to his ass and pull him impossibly tighter into my body. "Move!" I whisper urgently. "I need to feel you."

He groans and obliges, moving slowly inside me at first, and the sensation overwhelms me. I grab his face and yank him down into me, taking his mouth in a desperate kiss. It's like I can't get close enough to him. I want him to crawl inside me and live there.

I never want him to leave my body. It's completely overwhelming. He slides his hand down my chest, grabbing my cock again and stroking. Leaning back, he groans loudly and thrusts into me harder.

I reach the peak and topple over it, crying out as all of my muscles tense and my vision whites out. I feel Aleks tense and fall over his own peak right behind me, and we fall together into what feels like perfection.

CHAPTER 19
Ben

Monday morning, both Aleks and I are in the office early, but I still feel like I'm living in a dream. This week promises to be busy, getting ready for the game later this week where we'll be using the helmets for the first time in a real gameplay situation. I can't even believe it's finally happening, after so many years of hard work. We're really on the verge of something great here, I can feel it.

Truth be told though, the main reason I'm walking around with a smile so big it looks like I've got a coat hanger stuck in my mouth is because of Aleks Warren. I'm completely gone for him. And I'm so fucked.

The rest of our weekend together was absolutely amazing. I mean, yeah, I've had plenty of relationships, but I've never been with someone where it feels so effortless. Like I don't have to put on any armor. Aleks is amazing, and he likes me. I know that sounds like something I should be standing in front of a mirror saying to myself while combing my blond toupee. "Goshdarnit, people like me," but it's weirdly true. There aren't a lot of people in the world who I can truly be myself with. No bullshit, just me. He lets me fuss over him and take care of things, which makes me feel needed. And... I've missed that, missed having someone to take care of. If I'm truly honest, I think I've been lonely for a while. I haven't wanted to admit it, but it's nice to have someone around. Someone to do things with. After spending the weekend together being all Christmassy and doing things I haven't done since I was a kid, I realized how nice it was to have someone to enjoy that stuff with. I mean, I have Declan, but spending a whole day picking out a Christmas tree isn't really something we would do together. And the fact that for some unknown reason I trust Aleks enough to let him be the one to take care of me, is like icing on this incredible cake.

Josie was released from the hospital yesterday morning, so we picked her up together, after I convinced him that getting her into my big SUV would be easier on her than trying to climb into his little Tesla. *What, it's true! No ulterior motive whatsoever...*

As Aleks predicted, Josie supervised the tree decorating from a comfortable position on the couch. I really like her. She's smart as a fucking whip and utterly fearless. I loved hearing some of her stories about Aleks from when they were kids, and even though I know she had a terrible home life, it was nice hearing some of her happy childhood memories, and it seems like Aleks appears in most of those. After decorating the tree, Josie napped on the couch while Aleks and I made cookies, and the woman must have been truly exhausted because although we tried to be quiet, we didn't succeed very well, especially when a frosting war broke out with the red and green icing for the sugar cookies. Since we were both completely covered in icing, we had no choice but to shower to clean off at one point, which may have led to some other, more *adult* activities, but thankfully, Josie was passed out for that bit.

We brought her home to her place in the afternoon, and when I watched how sweet and caring Aleks was with her, fussing and making sure she had everything she could possibly need, I felt like the grinch whose heart grew two sizes that day. How could I have ever thought this guy was an entitled asshole? He's one of the most generous, giving people I've ever come across.

After getting Josie settled, we took a drive around town to look at the Christmas lights on all the beautiful houses. Holding his hand across the center console of my car, stealing glances at him, and watching his eyes light up as he admired the lights felt like something I've been waiting for my entire life. It's like Aleks fills a hole in my life I hadn't even known was there. The warm feeling in my chest is something I could get used to, and the thought of not having him around makes something ache inside me.

I have no idea whether we could ever work out the messy history between our families. I still don't even think Aleks knows about the connection, about what Kent did to my dad. If we did decide to try to make a go of this thing, that would have to be dealt with, obviously. But right now, just for a short while, I'm going to allow myself to have this. To have him. I'm already too far in over my head to avoid getting hurt, so if I'm going to be heartbroken anyway, I may as well make it worthwhile.

After returning to his place, we gorged ourselves on more cookies and then ordered pizza for a "proper dinner," cuddled on his couch a little more, and then snuggled into his bed, where we enjoyed a long, leisurely fuck session and fell asleep in each other's arms, feeling perfectly sated and happy. It was one of the best weekends of my entire life.

Partway through the morning, I'm alone in my temporary office going through some emails when my cell rings. It's a number I don't recognize right away, but the area code is from Boston.

"Dr. Ben Jacobs speaking," I answer.

"Dr. Jacobs. How are you, young man?" Dennis Madsen's warm voice comes through the line, bringing a wide smile to my face.

"Dr. Madsen, hello! I'm so glad to hear from you!"

"Benjamin, if you don't start calling me Dennis the way I've been telling you to for the last ten years, I'm going to have to rip you a new one."

A snort of laughter escapes me. The old man and I have been going back and forth for years over how I should address him, and it's become our little joke.

"I've been meaning to call and thank you for recommending me to take over the keynote speech at the gala a couple of weeks ago. Not to mention the fact that I've been wondering how Rosemary is doing."

"I can't think of anyone else I would choose to take my place, so no thanks necessary. And Rosemary is doing quite well, all things considered," he says, the smile in his voice evident. "I heard your keynote went well, yes? And how about your helmet project?"

My stomach warms. Dennis Madsen has been one of my heroes for years. Almost as much as Bob. It feels so good to hear he's happy for me.

"The speech went very well, thanks. And you know how I struggle with public speaking, so that's saying something."

Dennis chuckles.

"And we'll be putting the helmets into an actual gameplay situation later this week with the Sasquatch," I say, a little flutter of pride floating around in my belly.

"That is wonderful, young man. From what I've seen, that helmet could revolutionize player safety for a whole new generation of athletes. You and your team should be very proud of yourselves." I can hear the smile in his voice, and it warms my heart. "But that's not why I called you today. I have something else I need to discuss with you," he says, his tone serious.

"Oh, what's going on?"

"Well, Ben, you and I have discussed a succession plan for my research and my lab when I'm ready to leave it. I know you've been quite interested in taking over when the time comes."

"Right," I say cautiously.

"So, it appears the time may be coming sooner than I'd planned. I need to start making arrangements for someone to assume responsibility for it as soon as possible."

"Wait, what?" I say, surprised. "I thought you weren't going to retire for at least five more years?"

"That was the plan, yes. But the universe apparently has other ideas," he says, and my stomach sinks.

"You're not—there's nothing wrong, is there?"

"No, no, not with me. My health is fine. But the reason I needed to stay home with Rosemary during your gala was because her breast cancer has returned after all these years."

"Oh, shit, Dennis, I'm so sorry." Dennis' wife, Rosemary, is like the other half of his whole. When I was living in Boston and he was my professor, she took it upon herself to be my stand-in mom, even though my parents visited regularly. She's one of the loveliest people I've ever met. I know she survived breast cancer many years ago, long before I met them, and the fact that it's come back doesn't sound good.

"Thank you, son. Fortunately, it's a good news, bad news situation. Yes, the cancer has returned, but the good news is that it's been caught early again, and they expect she'll be fine. But she's asked that I cut down my hours substantially. Not only while she's going through treatment but afterwards. We always said we were going to travel, and we just haven't done much. That's my fault, and I want to make sure we get to do those things before it's too late. This is a wake-up call for me. We're both seventy now, and by the time she's up to long trips again, we might be seventy-one or seventy-two. It's time to slow down and try to see more of the world than just the inside of this lab."

"Oh, Dennis. Wow, that's huge news. I mean, I'm glad her prognosis is so good. It sounds like you're making the right decision."

"Yes. That much, I know. Cutting back on the work is surprisingly one of the easiest decisions I've ever made. But of course, I will need to nominate someone to take over my lab. And Ben, I'm not going to beat around the bush. I'd like to nominate you."

"Oh, wow, I... Wow, that's... I'm honored," I say somewhat weakly as my mind spins. If Dennis had called with this news two months ago, I would have been over the moon with excitement. But things are... complicated now. There's my equipment project with the Sasquatch, and of course, there's Aleks.

"Now, I'm not the one who gets the final say in the matter. The university board holds all those cards. But from what I hear, your helmet trial out there with the Sasquatch is on their radar, and they're impressed with both the science and the fact that you've been able to get a professional sports league to agree to participate. That's been a roadblock for other researchers, as you're aware. I would say that if you can close out that data collection phase of the trial without any major incidents or disruptions, you'll be a shoo-in for the job."

"Right, of course. I understand," I say, feeling like I'm underwater. "That's amazing, Dennis. I hardly know what to say."

"It is sooner than we had planned, but I believe you're ready for this now, Ben. From what I've heard, it sounds like your stepfather's first few weeks on the new drug trial have been going well. I know he and your mom will be sad to see you leave the West Coast, but they'll be damn proud of you as well."

"Um, yes. Yeah. Yes, of course, they sure will. Wow, I'm just... Wow."

Dennis can obviously tell there's something not quite right with my reaction—the old man's nearly as perceptive as my mother. "What is it, son?" I can hear the concern in his voice.

"No, nothing. Honestly, Dennis, I'm just blindsided. What kind of timing are you thinking about?"

"Well, like I said, I think if you can get the data collection phase covered while you're there, you should be able to tackle the analysis in the lab here. I'll leave the ultimate decision up to you, of course, but I would think that by early in the new year, you should be able to make the move, yes?"

"Yeah, no, I mean, yes, of course. That makes sense."

"Now, timing-wise, there is a meeting of the board of trustees this week, and I think it would be extremely helpful if you could come out and attend it with me. I apologize for the short notice on that, but I think it will make a huge difference if they have the chance to meet you personally. Frankly, I think that will probably lock the whole thing down for you, and you'll be able to make your plans."

I give my head a shake. This is the opportunity I've been waiting for my entire career. Taking over Dr. Madsen's lab has been my goal since I knew what it was. There's no other research facility like it in the field of neuroscience.

There's no way I can turn down this kind of opportunity. Is there?

"Yes, um, I'm sure I can make that happen, Dennis. I'll just need to confirm a couple of things first." I clear my throat. "This is an incredible opportunity, Dennis. I'm... I'm so honored. Thank you so much. It means so much to me."

His voice is warm and kind. "I know it does, son. I know you'll do great work here. There is no one else I'd be so comfortable leaving my research to. And I'll be around a while longer. I'm sure I won't be able to ditch the life completely. Rosemary knows that too." He chuckles. "But now it will be you catching me up on all the cutting-edge discoveries, not the other way around. I can't wait to see what you'll accomplish here."

We end the call with him promising to send me some documents I need to fill out so he can officially nominate me to the university chancellor before the upcoming meeting. It should be straightforward since I'm a former student, and according to Dennis, there's no one he's working with right now who wants to take his place, as they're all heads down in their own research. It means I should be able to transition smoothly into the role, which is great. But... fuck. *Why am I not happy about this? And more importantly, what the hell am I going to do about Aleks?*

CHAPTER 20
Aleks

W alking into the offices adjacent to the Sasquatch's rink on Monday morning, I still feel like I'm walking on air. Even with Josie's accident, this turned into one of the best weekends of my entire life. The three of us had such an amazing time yesterday after we brought Jo back to my place from the hospital. Even though she was tired and still feeling pretty shitty, we had her laughing, and she and Ben got along perfectly. I haven't had a chance to talk with her alone since Ben and I were, um, otherwise occupied for the rest of the evening after we got her settled at home, but my plan is to drop in on her after work today.

After a productive morning and lunch with some of the equipment techs, I find some time to speak with Carson, needing to touch base on the helmet project and also wanting to thank him in person for pushing all my team benefits through so quickly. Josie was super appreciative when I told her the team had offered to cover all her home care costs and anything else she needs. Jo does okay with money—she has a healthy inheritance from her grandmother, plus her own job—but because of her terrible upbringing, she's very cautious. Honestly, I can't blame her. This gesture from the team means she won't have to fight with her insurance company to get the expenses like home nursing care covered, which is a huge load off her shoulders. It means even more since, legally speaking, we're not technically "family," but Carson worked some magic to get her covered underneath my plan.

After waving hello to Kelly, who's on the phone, I make my way down the hall to his office. It's unusual for a team's GM to have such an open-door policy, but Carson is always saying to drop in anytime. He even made that clear to those of us working for the EC Eagles, which says a lot about the kind of manager he is.

His door is slightly ajar, and as I get closer, I hear Carson speaking and another voice that sounds suspiciously like my dad, which is odd. I can't think of any reason for him to be here. I didn't even know they knew each other. I mean, Dad knows all the GMs in the league, but he doesn't usually make a habit of dropping in for visits.

I'm about to poke my head into the office to see what's going on when Dad says something that makes me freeze in my tracks, my stomach dropping.

"Look, Carson, I can see why you'd want to be first out of the gate with this kind of thing. I mean, talking about player safety is all the rage these days, I get it. But do you honestly think it's smart to mess with equipment midseason, especially when you guys are poised to make a playoff run? I mean, for god's sake, you're a first-year team—there's no damn way you should even be close to making the playoffs, let alone be sitting at the top of the division in December! It's fucking crazy, and if you want my advice, you absolutely can't take any chances on fucking that up."

"I hear what you're saying, Kent," Carson says. "And I appreciate your input, but we want to be on the cutting edge of player safety here at the Sasquatch. We're not planning to force any player to wear the new helmet if they're not comfortable, but so far, everyone is on board."

I can see the outline of my dad through the frosted glass windows of the office. He's sitting in one of the chairs on the other side of Carson's desk, his leg bouncing the way it often does when he's anxious.

"Look, Carson, I'm gonna be straight with you here. This is a mistake," my dad says, and my jaw drops. I can't believe what I'm hearing. I mean, I know my dad thinks CTE is unrelated to hits from hockey, but what possible reason would he have for trying to stop the Sasquatch from participating in this initiative? Especially when he knows this is my project. It's important to me, to the success of my career. *What the hell is happening here?*

From where I'm standing, I can only see a small sliver of the room, and I know I should get the hell out of here. I'm eavesdropping on a conversation I'm obviously not meant to hear, but I'm rooted to my spot. Suddenly, Dad gets up from his chair, and his fuzzy outline paces back and forth in front of the desk. With his chair empty, I can see a second person sitting in the other chair, and I have to stifle my gasp because it's Ben.

"Trust me on this," my dad is saying, his voice rapidly reaching an uncomfortable decibel level. "You don't want to rock the boat. A stupid helmet isn't going to stop concussions anyway. The game moves too fast. Protection can improve, but injuries are still going to happen. Trust me, you put some shiny new helmet on those veterans, and you'll have a rebellion of the old guard on your hands."

"Kent, with all due respect, this initiative isn't about the old guard. It's about keeping all our players as safe as possible," Carson says. "It's also about the future, and even keeping kids who play the game safe so their parents will let them play hockey and other contact sports." His voice is calm and measured, but it doesn't seem to be having any effect on my dad, who is clearly getting more and more angry.

Suddenly, Dad whirls around so he's facing Ben, his back to me. The tension in his shoulders is obvious, even through the frosted glass. "And then there's *you*!" he shouts. "How the fuck do you know anything? Have you ever played pro hockey? Taken a hit so hard you see stars and then bounced back up and kept playing because it's important? Because *winning fucking matters*, and you're there for the men on your team? Huh? Have you? I fuckin' doubt it. The only thing you're doing with this so-called 'safety initiative' is putting bullshit ideas in my son's head that the sport is 'dangerous.' You're making him lose respect for his old man and the game that gave him a very comfortable life. And do you know how I was able to give him that life? By being the meanest, toughest fucker out there, scrapping every fucking night. But you and your kind have been turning all our young men against that kind of life, making all of them believe they're too good to play that kind of game, that they're above all that, when the truth is you're all just using them. You're using Aleks and all the other young guys out there so you and your lab coat buddies can get your names in the news or in some fancy medical journal." He pauses for breath before continuing, and I can picture the enraged look on his face; I've seen it many times when he gets going on a rant. But what comes out of his mouth is something I haven't heard before, and it cuts me to the quick.

"Look, Aleks is so fuckin' desperate for a way into management in this league he'll latch onto any crazy idea if he thinks it will attract attention. He can't see that this is all a waste of money and resources. Aleks is a good kid, but he's too idealistic—his head's in the fuckin clouds. He can't see this so-called research of yours trying to link hockey and brain damage is just hogwash. You're all just a bunch of damn lab coats trying to vilify hockey. There's no solid proof of what you're saying, and in the meantime, you're destroying the legacies of generations of guys who shed blood, sweat, and teeth on the ice purely for the love of the game and the love of their teammates. It's all just bullshit." My dad is panting. Meanwhile, I feel like I've been stabbed by someone who should be my biggest supporter.

"Kent, I'm only going to say this once," Ben says in a tone I've never heard from him. His voice cuts like a blade, and frankly, it's a little bit scary and a whole lot of hot. "I care about your son, and I refuse to listen to you talk down about him. Aleks is smart as hell, and while he might have high ideals, he is not naïve. He's not going to have any problem making it in this league—you don't need to worry about that. The condescending way you're talking about him right now is the only bullshit I can detect in this office. You'd better give your head a shake, Kent, and start treating your son with the respect he deserves because if you don't, your precious legacy as a hockey player won't be the only thing you'll lose in this battle."

"Now, listen here—" my dad says, but Ben cuts him off, and *ho-lee shitballs*, the way he's standing up to my dad and defending me is making me all hot and bothered. *Is that weird?*

"Excuse me, I'm not finished yet," Ben says, and I nearly swoon. "As for your feelings about my research, you're entitled to your opinion, but you don't get to come into this office and insult me, my research team, Carson, and least of all your son." He clears his throat before continuing, and I'm pretty sure the only reason my dad isn't losing his shit right now is because he's so surprised at the way Ben is standing up to him. "Now, in response to your question about whether I've played pro hockey, the answer, as you're aware, is no, I have not. However, it seems like you may not know that I *do* have *very* personal experience with life as a hockey player, and I know *exactly* what kind of damage it can do to another person. My stepfather is Bob Prescott."

Dad gasps, and the room is silent. I'm confused though. I'm sure Dad knows who Bob Prescott is, since they played at the same time, but I don't understand why Ben brought up his stepdad's name like he's some kind of weapon.

The next person to speak is my father, and his voice is shaky. "I... I didn't realize Bob was your stepfather. Does... does Aleks know?" Now I'm really even more confused. *Do I know what? And why does Dad sound so shaken up?*

"I've mentioned who my dad is, but I don't think Aleks realizes the... connection... you two have," Ben says.

The room goes silent again, and I can hear my father breathing heavily. *What in the hell is he so upset about? What is this connection he has to Ben's stepfather?*

Carson speaks next, and his voice is gentle but firm. "Look, gentlemen, I think we've gotten off track here. Kent, I know it's probably not easy to watch the game you love change so dramatically, but if we don't move forward, we're going to become extinct. I get that maybe it's not the perfect time to run a project of this nature, given that we're doing so much better as a first-year team than anyone could have predicted. I'll discuss it again with the coaching staff to make sure they're still on board because those concerns are valid. But regardless of when it happens, this initiative is going ahead, Kent."

There's another pause, and I realize I'm still standing outside Carson's office, eavesdropping like a creeper. I turn to tiptoe back down the hall, but before I'm out of earshot, I hear Carson say one last thing. "Honestly, Kent, I'm not sure why you're so adamantly against this. This project is an excellent opportunity for your son. And personally, I think Aleks is going to knock this out of the park."

My head spins as I make my way quietly back down the hall. As much as I'm thrilled that Carson is happy with the job I'm doing, my heart aches from my dad's betrayal. Thankfully, Kelly isn't at their desk, so I don't have to come up with an excuse for sneaking out, and I slip into the stairwell instead of waiting for the elevator.

What the actual fuck was that all about? Clearly, there's something going on between my family and Ben's that I don't know about, and it's time everyone stops keeping it from me.

CHAPTER 21

Ben

The confrontation with Kent Warren shocked the shit out of me, but maybe it was inevitable. After finishing my call with Dennis, I'd gone up to meet with Carson about the job offer in Boston. I'd tried desperately to contact Aleks to talk to him first, but he was swamped with the other equipment techs, and there was no time. Dennis had already contacted the university board, letting them know I was going to come to Boston to meet with them in a few days, so I needed to speak to Carson right away in case, somehow, word got out. Even though that was unlikely, I didn't want to take the chance that he heard about it from anyone but me. I wouldn't want him to hear it from anyone but me. When I reached his office, Kent Warren was in there, and they were already deep into a discussion about why Kent thinks the helmet safety project is a bad idea. I don't know who the fuck he thinks he is. He's not affiliated with the Sasquatch in any official way, and I don't even know what his job is with the league, other than he's some kind of special advisor to the league governors. Whatever his job is, I don't think it gives him any right to blow into the Sasquatch's office and talk down to their GM and disparage my work and that of my research team. On top of that, he talked a lot of shit about his own son, making Aleks sound like some kind of childish fool, and I nearly saw red he made me so angry.

I couldn't help the sense of smug satisfaction when Kent reacted with shock to finding out I'm related to Bob. But that feeling was short-lived. It was replaced very quickly with a feeling of deep sadness because the more Kent dug in his heels, the less likely it became that there could ever be a chance for Aleks and me.

The thought of letting him go curdles my stomach. I'm pretty sure I've already started falling in love with Aleks Warren, but I just can't see how it could work. The bitterness and bad blood between our families would mean we would be starting off in a bad place. Add to that the fact that we would be trying to navigate a long-distance relationship, and I just think we're doomed. Better for both of us to cut things off now rather than drag it out for months, hurting us both even more in the process.

When I get to his place after work, it's obvious he's got something on his mind, but he doesn't bring it up until after we've eaten and are sitting on his couch, each with a beer. There's an uneasy feeling hanging between us, thick as a heavy curtain.

"We need to talk," we both say at the same time, and our eyes meet in surprise before we both laugh, helping to diffuse some of the tension in the room.

"I overheard a conversation today in Carson's office," Aleks begins, and my eyebrows shoot up. *Oh my god, did he hear me talking to Carson about the Boston job?* After Kent left, I stayed to discuss my job situation and told him I was moving to Boston.

"I know I shouldn't have listened, but I was going in to thank him for everything with Josie, and I heard you all talking," Aleks says. "I apologize for eavesdropping on you." He clears his throat, looking down to where he's peeling the label off his beer bottle. "But I want to thank you for standing up for me to my father. He can be... difficult. I appreciate what you said about me, so thank you." He finally shifts his gaze so his eyes meet mine, and they're filled with uncertainty.

"You're welcome," I say, reaching for his hand. Maybe he didn't hear the conversation that happened after Kent left. "I meant what I said. You're an amazing person, and you deserve respect. Your dad seems to have trouble with that." I clear my own throat. "Um, but I... I need to talk to you about—"

He bites his lip, looking back down at where our hands are clasped. "Hold on, okay? Can you let me finish first?" He looks at me, and there's something in his green eyes I can't decipher. I'm not sure if it's curiosity or something else.

"Of course. I'm sorry, go ahead," I say, and he continues.

"So, I'm sorry for my father's meddling. I don't know why he's so hell-bent on trying to stop this project. And I'm going to talk to him about it. But first, I... ahem, I really need to know what you were talking about when you said there was a connection between my dad and yours? Something obviously happened between them."

Sucking in a deep breath, I close my eyes for a moment, trying to gather my strength. This is going to be so hard. *I want Aleks, I don't want to hurt my family, and I want my dream job. How is this going to work?*

I let go of his hands and stand, needing physical space so I can explain everything without getting distracted. I pace back and forth in front of his coffee table, rubbing the back of my neck with one hand, no longer able to meet his eyes.

"So, Jesus, Aleks, there's a lot of stuff I need to unpack here." I let out a heavy sigh. "So, I'll start at the beginning. I... I haven't been totally transparent with you, and I'm sorry about that."

"Um... What? What's that supposed to mean?" he asks.

"That first night we were together a few weeks ago... The reason I ran off on you that night was because I saw one of your family photos, and I figured out Kent Warren is your father."

He cocks his head. "Okay. Does this have something to do with this mysterious connection between my dad and your stepdad?"

"Yeah. It does." I rub the back of my neck again. I feel strange telling Aleks this story when it's something he should probably hear from his own father, but regardless, I owe him an explanation because it's affected my own behavior. "So, our dads played together back in the day. They were teammates at one point, but for most of their careers, they weren't on the same team, and Bob was an enforcer, same as your dad. So, they fought. A lot."

He looks at me with confusion. "Okay. And?"

"It was part of the game then, obviously, but what you don't know is that the main reason my stepdad has dementia, the reason he's in that care facility and he's barely even sixty years old, is, at least partially, because of the final hit he took. He was knocked out cold on the ice, and he had to be in the hospital for several days after a really intense hit. Your dad was the one who hit him. It ended Bob's hockey career. He never played again after that."

Aleks's expression morphs into genuine sorrow and then into understanding. "Oh. Oh... I didn't know that. Fuck. That's awful. I'm so sorry." He chews on the inside of his cheek. "That's why my dad was so surprised when you told him you're Bob's stepson to-day? Because there's this thing that happened between them a long time ago?"

"Well, I..." I sigh. "Obviously, I don't know what was going on in your dad's head, but he didn't know that I'm Bob's son, so he probably assumed I wasn't aware of the story and what went down between them."

He furrows his brows. "Um. Okay? I'm still kinda confused though. It was something that happened in a game, right?"

"Oh yeah, it all happened during the game. But the hit was controversial. It was ruled legal during the game, but the league reviewed it carefully afterward, and back then, they didn't really do that. It's not like today where they have a whole disciplinary committee and stuff. So, for them to look at this hit after the game was over, this was a pretty big deal at the time. Anyway, a lot of people believe it was way, way over the line. For a time, there were rumors that the police were going to charge your dad with assault, but that never went anywhere. And my dad still has some hard feelings about it."

Aleks' eyes widen in surprise. "Oh. Oh. I see... So, it was pretty violent, I guess?" Aleks chews on his lip.

"Yeah. I don't want to overplay it or anything, but it's still the most vicious hit I've ever seen in a hockey game," I say quietly.

"Oh, wow," he says softly. "I've—obviously, I know my dad was a big hitter, but I don't know why I didn't know about this. I've even watched a few of his old highlight reels from back in the day when they used to celebrate the biggest hits of the year, but no one's ever mentioned this one to me. My father's certainly never talked about it." Aleks looks both sad and confused. "How could I not know?"

"They don't include that hit in those kinds of collections of the big hits and stuff because of the severity of the injury," I say. I don't want him to blame himself for not knowing about something that happened when he was just a child. "There are other big hits and fights that don't appear. It's like the league would just prefer they all go away quietly so people forget all about them. If you looked it up specifically, you'd find footage, but if you didn't know it happened, I can see why you'd never have done that."

Aleks chews on his lip. "I still don't know why my dad wouldn't have mentioned it. Especially once I started working on this safety project."

"Maybe it's not something he's proud of, I don't know." Fuck, I hope he's not proud of it. But from the way he handled everything after the fact, it's hard to tell.

"So, at least I know what you meant now." Aleks is quiet for a moment, and an uncomfortable silence hangs between us.

"There's probably more we can talk about related to that, but you probably want to talk with your dad about it first. Hear his side of what happened," I say. "But I, um, I have something else I need to talk to you about."

"Oh, right. I'm sorry. Go ahead." He gives me a weak smile, clearly a little shaken by what he's just learned.

I take a deep breath because this is going to hurt. "I got a call today from my old professor at Boston University. The one who I stood in for at the gala."

Aleks nods. "Oh yeah? How did that go?"

I'm going to have to just spit this out, otherwise I won't be able to get through it. "I, um, well, you know how my goal is to take over his lab someday?" Aleks nods. "Right, so, um. He called me today to tell me he's going to retire earlier than he thought. Like, now. And he wants me to take over his lab and his research. So, if I'm awarded the position by the university, I'll have to move to Boston." My voice cracks on the last word, and I clear my throat, trying valiantly to keep my shit together.

Aleks looks at me like he's been slapped, and I nearly break right then and there. He gulps. "Oh. Wow. You're moving?" He closes his eyes and repeats himself, only this time, it's a statement, not a question. "You're moving." Taking a deep breath, he opens his eyes. "Right. Right. Um. When... When will you be going?"

"I don't know exactly. Dennis said they want someone in the position as soon as possible. I'm not sure why—some university politics or something." I pause. "But it will be soon. Early in the new year."

"Oh." Aleks' face is shuttered, closed off, but then he turns to me with a heartbreaking look in his green eyes.

"I think I hear what you're saying, Ben." His voice is barely above a whisper. "This isn't going to work, is it?"

Every part of my being wants to argue with him, to tell him he's crazy, that of course we can figure out a way to make things work between us. But I know I can't. It wouldn't be fair because it's not the truth. The ugly truth is that there really is no realistic way forward for us.

"I—" My voice breaks, so I clear my throat again and start over. *Fuck, this hurts.* "I want it to work, but I just don't see a way. Trying to manage a long-distance relationship is so hard, and then there's my family. I—they've been through so much already, you know? I can't..."

"You can't bring yourself to add more stress onto them. And if we were together, it would be stressful." Aleks nods slowly, almost talking to himself. "Because of me. Because I'm a reminder of that shitty thing that happened to your dad. The shitty thing my father did to him."

I nod once, hating every second of this. "And, you know, you're going to be so busy here with the team. The Sasquatch love you already, and you're going to be such a star within the organization. I just know you're going to be amazing, no matter what you end up doing." My voice is rough, and I swipe a couple of stray tears off my cheeks.

Aleks nods. "You're probably right. Better to end things now than draw it out for six months or a year and then figure it out. That would be worse." His voice is shaky, but when I look into his eyes, they're shuttered, like a wall has slammed down, and I don't have access to that part of him anymore. My heart cracks open even wider.

"For what it's worth, Aleks, I'm... If things were different, I think we could be something."

"Yeah." He smiles sadly. "Yeah. I do too. I'm sorry."

"I'm sorry too," I whisper, and I open my arms for him one last time. He comes in for a hug, tentatively at first, but it morphs into something more. Like we're desperate to memorize every second of how this feels because we both know it's the last time.

After standing there for who knows how long, clinging to each other with tears streaming down our faces, I gather my things and slip out the door of his loft. As I start my car, I look up to where his windows overlook the snowy street and see his silhouette there, watching as I get into my car. I hold up one hand in a sort of wave before I drive off, forcing myself not to look back.

CHAPTER 22
Aleks

My heart shatters as the door clicks shut softly behind Ben. But underneath the raw heartbreak, a seething anger directed at my father starts bubbling up. I'm furious about the cowardly way he handled that game against Bob's team years ago and for his selfishness in keeping it from me. His actions, both past and present, fuel my rage, and suddenly, my loft feels like a prison as I pace back and forth. I can't wait any longer to confront him. This conversation needs to happen right fucking now.

I call Josie on my way out to my parents. As expected, she's totally supportive. "Absolutely, you need to go over there right now!" she says confidently when I ask her if I'm acting like a lunatic. "Look, A, we both know your dad has his faults. God knows Kent Warren isn't an easy man. But, hon, I really do believe he loves you. I don't know what the hell was going through his head when he was talking shit about you in that meeting today, but every time I've heard him talk about you, *ever*, he's always been *so* proud of you. He's always talking about how smart and driven you are. I know he never shows that to you, and I promise, I'm not just saying it because of what your parents did for me and how much I love them." Josie takes a breath before continuing. "This is a terrible thing to say about someone who saved my life, but hon, Kent Warren has the maturity level of a fourteen-year-old boy. He has the emotional depth of a kiddie pool and enough testosterone to power a rock concert, but he's not a bad person, and he loves you. I have no idea why he would be trying to fuck up this project, but you're doing the right thing by talking to him. Maybe this will be a chance for you guys to, I don't know, maybe have a different kind of relationship."

"Maybe," I say, feeling doubtful about this being good in any way for my relationship with my father. "I don't know, but I just pulled up to their place, so I'm gonna go see what he has to say for himself." I pull into the curved driveway of my parent's ostentatious mansion. The outdoor lights are on, but from what I can see, the rest of the house is dark. Not surprising. My parents often go to bed super early.

"Good luck, hon. You've got this. I love you." Josie says, and I nod, even though she can't see me.

"Yeah. I'm good. I got this. Thanks, Jo. I'll call you."

I end the call as always, eternally grateful for my best friend's incredible strength. But now it's time to confront the lion in his den. I let myself in using the coded keypad, so if they're awake, they'll get the message that it was my code that opened the door. Sure enough, a moment later, I hear my father call out from their room upstairs, and a minute later, he comes down the massive, curved staircase.

"Aleks? What's going on, son?" he says, a tinge of panic in his voice.

My mom is right behind him. "Aleksandr, is everything alright? What are you doing here unexpectedly?"

"I'm fine, Mom. Nothing's wrong. I just really need to speak with Dad, and it couldn't wait." They both give me confused looks. My dad is now at the bottom of the stairway, standing a couple of feet in front of me, and my mom stands halfway up, clutching her silk robe in one hand and the banister in the other. She descends the remaining stairs more slowly and comes to stand in front of me, hitting the light switch on her way. Reaching out, she puts her hands on my biceps and holds me away from her, giving me a motherly once-over to make sure I'm not physically hurt before pulling me into a crushing hug. My mother might not be perfect, but I've never doubted for one second how much she loves me. And she really does give the best hugs—she hugs you like she really means it.

I allow myself to relax in her warmth for just a moment before straightening up. "I'm fine, Mom, I promise. But I really need to talk with Dad about something important."

She looks at me again and cocks an eyebrow like she's not quite sure whether to believe me, but seeing as I appear to be physically intact, I guess she decides to let it go. "Okay. But you scared us," she says a bit reproachfully before giving me a kiss on my cheek and another quick squeeze. As she turns to go back upstairs, she and my dad exchange a glance, communicating in that way people who've been married for a long time do. She's asking Dad what the hell this is all about, and he's telling her he's got no idea.

As she heads back up the staircase, I turn to face my father, and for some reason, the edge of unease I often have around him isn't there. Right now, I'm as calm, cool, and collected as a goddamn cucumber, despite the anger coursing through me.

"What's this about, son?" he asks.

"I have to talk to you, Dad. We should sit down."

He bobs his head. "Alright, let's go in my den." He turns to lead us down the hallway, but something inside me resists that idea. I don't want to have this conversation in his den. That ultra-masculine lair of his that has always made me feel uncomfortable.

"No, Dad. Let's go in the kitchen," I say, and there's surprise on his face as he turns around.

"Okay, ah, sure," he says and follows me into the kitchen, where I pull out one of the heavy wooden chairs gathered around the long table.

Once we're sitting down, I take a deep breath. There's no way I'm chickening out of this now. The problem is, I'm not exactly sure what I want to hear from him.

"Dad, I overheard you talking with Carson and Ben today in Carson's office."

His eyes widen. "How did you hear that?"

I let out a bitter laugh. "I went to talk to Carson about something and just about walked in on you. Instead, I overheard everything, including the way you were talking about me."

At least he has the decency to look ashamed. He doesn't meet my eyes as he swallows hard. "Look, son..." He clears his throat. "I was just concerned for the sake of the team. You know all that CTE stuff is just silly. This whole thing is like some kind of little science project for these egghead doctors. Plus, it's like I told you, coaches from my generation are going to have a lot of concerns about this technology being added to the game. There's a fine line between doing what's reasonable and possibly affecting the integrity of the game."

He pauses for a minute, his eyes darting to the side, and I can literally feel my blood pressure rising. "Nope. No way, Dad. This isn't about the 'integrity of the game.' I'm not letting you use those stupid talking points on me. Maybe you really do feel that way, but you wouldn't make your son look like a foolish child in front of his *boss* just because you're worried about that. *Would you*?"

He tries to interrupt me, but I forge ahead. "Now, while you've never bothered to tell me this yourself, others tell me that you're actually rather proud of me, even though I find that hard to believe. But for you to be talking shit about me like that, there's got to be more to it than just your 'integrity of the game' line. Oh, and just so you know, Ben Jacobs and I have been seeing each other, but he ended things with me tonight. You wanna know why he broke it off with me? He doesn't think we stand a chance due to the fact that you ended his stepfather's hockey career with a borderline criminally illegal hit and never even bothered to acknowledge it, never even bothered to talk to him, after it happened."

The color drains from my father's face. "Oh" is the only thing that comes out of his mouth. He looks at me for a minute before speaking again. "Aleks, I'm sorry. Obviously, I didn't know."

"What is it that you're sorry for, Dad? Are you sorry I overheard the shit you said about me, trying to make me look stupid for your own gain? Or are you saying you're sorry for never telling me that you were almost charged with assault for that hit you laid on Bob Prescott? Even when I told you about my new project, the one that finally got me my *dream job* on an NHL team, a project trying to prevent *exactly* the same kind of injuries you gave Bob Prescott, you still didn't think I should know that story?" I'm on a roll now, my anger starting to bubble over. "Or is it that you're sorry for the way you handled it in the first place? Like how you never even fucking bothered to reach out to Bob Prescott after you forced him into an early retirement! Tell me, Dad, what exactly is it you're sorry for?"

As I make it through my tirade, it's almost like I can see the image my dad has of me changing as I speak. It's possible, just maybe, for the first time ever, my father is seeing me as a grown man instead of an extension of himself who never lived up to what was expected of him.

The most surprising thing though, as I stand there demanding some accountability from him, is that maybe, for the first time in *my* own life, I feel like my own man. Someone separate from the legendary NHL bruiser Kent Warren. I'm nothing like that guy: the fighter, the enforcer that was my father during his playing days. But his whole identity is wrapped up in that persona, and I can finally see it clearly. All of my brothers and me, and probably even Christine, to some extent, have been measured against that version of my dad. Not only by the outside world but by *him*. That's what he wanted and what he still wants: for us to continue doing what he loved once he got too old. He wants to live vicariously through us because he doesn't know any other way to value himself. But it's never fucking mattered what we actually want for ourselves.

All of these thoughts swirl through my mind in a jumbled mess as I wait for him to answer.

He sucks in a breath and squares his shoulders, but somehow, he still looks smaller to me than he did a few minutes ago.

"I'm sorry for a lot of things, son. Right now, I'm sorry I hurt you."

That takes some of the wind out of my sails. "Why, Dad? Why the hell would you talk about me that way? This is an important project for my career. Why would you try to make me look stupid? I don't understand." Part of me feels like I should be ripping him a new one over what he did. But instead of rage, it's waves of disappointment and sadness that swamp me.

Something in my tone must disarm my dad, taking all the fight out of him, because it's like he deflates before my eyes. He leans forward, elbows on the table, and holds his head in his hands.

"Look, Aleks, it's complicated, alright? I've been so consumed with getting you taken off that project because I... It's... I don't know how to handle any of this. I played in the league for twenty years. I fought almost every single game I played. Do you know how many times I knocked guys out cold? I mean, Jesus Christ, it was almost every damn night of my life." He gets up from his chair, getting a glass and filling it with cold water from the fridge dispenser, his hand shaking.

"That hit against Bob Prescott is one of my deepest regrets. It was... fuck, it was vicious and brutal. Everything they said about it was true. It was an evil thing that I did."

"What happened, Dad? Why did you do it? You weren't a dirty player, I know that."

He shakes his head. "For what it's worth, it was supposed to be payback for a hit Bob laid on one of our stars in a game a few weeks earlier. Steve Youngston. It wasn't a dirty hit, but it was hard, and it took one of our top scorers out of the lineup for several weeks while he healed up. And you know what it was like in those days. Coach decided there would be payback, one way or another. But that game was one of those nights. We were getting our asses handed to us." He shakes his head, his eyes looking into space as if he's seeing the game even now. "We were down four goals, and it was nearing the end of the third period, so we had no hope of catching up. I was angry. Angry at losing, angry at Bob for taking out Steve and fucking up our chances at the playoffs, and honestly, I was an angry young man in those days. How fucking stupid, right?" He grimaces. "I had everything a man could want. I had a beautiful family, a wonderful wife, more money than I could have ever dreamed of... I had no reason to be angry, but I still was back then." He clears his throat and takes a sip of water before continuing.

"Anyway, there were only a few minutes left in the third, and the coach told me to go for it. And I did. They put me on the ice, and I fucking went for Bob. The crowd was anticipating it; it had been brewing for the whole game. I mean, it had been brewing since that hit on Youngston a few weeks earlier, but I came at Bob from behind with a vicious cross-check. He went down and never got back up. It was sickening, Aleks. I don't know if you've watched the footage, but it's fucking shameful. I'll never, ever forgive myself for it."

He takes a shaky breath. "And your next question is probably going to be why didn't I reach out to him, right? Why didn't I apologize in person? At least show him some respect, after I had disrespected him as another human being so disgracefully?"

I nod, chewing on my lip, because of course, that was exactly what my next question was going to be.

"The truth is, I followed advice from my shitty lawyers and the league lawyers. I knew it was wrong—fuck, I actually wanted to go to the hospital that night, but they talked me out of it. And I let them talk me out of it, and I kept letting them talk me out of reaching out to him because I knew. Aleks, I knew I'd fucked him up badly. I knew it the second it happened. And I wanted them to talk me out of trying to apologize to him. Because I knew I'd done wrong, and I was completely fucking terrified. I thought I might go to jail. I thought I might be banned from the league... But that doesn't matter. I still should have reached out, and I'm sorry I never did."

He sighs. "It's the worst, most shameful thing I've done in my life, Aleks. And it breaks my fuckin' heart that my shitty behavior is still having terrible consequences even this many years later."

"Dad..." I'm stunned. This is not how I thought this conversation was going to go.

"Anyway. This shit... this... evidence... linking brain damage and hockey has been coming out for years. And I've spent all that time trying so hard not to think about it because I haven't been able to face the possibility of..." His voice cracks. "The possibility that I might be responsible for doing that kind of damage to guys. We used to fight because it was our job. I know you get that, but these guys, Aleks, these are *my people.* What if it turns out that the reason these men are suffering now is because of *me*, because of the way I beat the shit out of them so many goddamn times?" He blows out a breath, and my heart breaks for my dad. I never knew he had feelings this deep, not about anything. But he keeps talking.

"I never once pulled a punch, never held back. Never once. And they gave me awards for it. I got awards for the most knockouts, the hardest hit, all that kind of crap." He lets out a choked noise that's somewhere between a hysterical laugh and a sob. "And the most messed-up thing is I don't have it. I don't have the headaches, the memory problems or flashbacks they talk about. I'm fucking fine, yet all these guys are losing their minds? I can't..."

I sit stunned as my father chokes back another sob. I don't know what to say.

He sits back down in the chair across from me and sucks in a deep breath, trying to control his emotions. "When you told me you were going to be working on this project, I sort of panicked. I didn't want you to know how much damage I've done in this world.

How many people I hurt and how many lives I destroyed. And fuck, when Ben Jacobs told me his step-dad is Bob Prescott—" He swallows. "—I think I knew it was all over right then." He shakes his head. "I still can't stand the thought that you might be ashamed of me."

"But Dad," I say gently. "Even if I never found out about that hit, Brad and Mike play. They must know about it, right? And Chrissy too?"

"Your brothers and sister... I'm sure they know. We've never talked about it." He gets up from the table again, pacing back and forth like some kind of trapped animal while twisting his wedding band around his finger. "But they're just... They're more like me. Even if they do know about it, they'd never think of coming to me demanding answers, asking me to explain why I did what I did to Bob Prescott. You're different, Aleks, you always have been. You're so much more sophisticated, so much smarter than any of us. My god, son, I knew you were the smartest person in this family by the time you were out of diapers. And when you stopped playing hockey, it was like the last thing we had in common disappeared. Even though you were only a kid, I knew I'd never be able to keep up with you. You're fucking brilliant and determined, and you're such a good man, Aleks. I've always known that if you knew about what I did to Bob Prescott, you'd ask questions." He smiles wryly. "And I never wanted to have to answer them."

Looking at him in the dim light, my father looks way older than his fifty-nine years. He looks like a small old man regretting his life choices, and my heart breaks a little more for him.

"Dad, back in those days, no one knew how much damage you all were doing to each other. It was a different time. Plus, you weren't the only guy in the league to dish out big hits and hard punches. You can't seriously be trying to shoulder all this blame yourself."

He shakes his head. "I know, but it doesn't excuse what I did. I had an awful lot of rage, and I took it out on those guys every night. It was so much easier to do that than to face all my personal issues."

I've never seen my dad show one sign of weakness, ever, in my whole life. I never once suspected his hard exterior concealed so much guilt. The great and fearsome Kent Warren has a soft underbelly?

"Dad, you can't carry all this guilt. It's like what you were saying – you were doing your job – getting paid to kick guys' asses."

He gives me a sad smile. "It's okay, Aleks. I'm sorry I've laid all of this on you, and I'm so sorry for trying to screw up your project. I'll do my best to make things right." He pauses, scraping his hand through his hair. "And, I hope you believe me, but I truly didn't know you were seeing the doctor. I... I'm sorry I fucked that up for you too."

I let out a sigh. "Yeah. I mean, that's not... There are other reasons Ben and I can't be together. But I'm glad I finally know where you're coming from on this CTE denial. But Dad, I think you should talk with someone; you shouldn't be carrying all the guilt on your own. That's not fair. You had an amazing career, and you should be proud of it. The world is just different now."

We both stand, and I give my dad a hug, a real one, not some half-assed bro-hug. It's something we haven't done in forever, and he holds me tightly for a moment.

"Aleks, I'm *so fucking* proud of you, son. I know I don't show it the right way, but please don't ever doubt that. I love you so much."

I swallow the lump in my throat. "Thanks, Dad. I appreciate you saying that. I love you too. But I, um, I should go."

We say goodbye, and I'm still reeling from the conversation as I drive home. I went there expecting a huge confrontation, and instead, I got to see a side of my father I never knew existed. And while I'm glad I know what happened now, I still have no idea if there's anything I can do to make things right with Ben.

CHAPTER 23
Aleks

C hrist, it's been a long few days, but tonight is the night Ben's helmets are going to be worn during real gameplay. And the worst part of it is that Ben isn't even here to see it, although maybe that's a good thing for me. I'm not sure I'd be able to keep my shit together if he was here. Instead, two of the guys from his team are here to make sure everything goes smoothly.

He texted me yesterday to say he was in Boston to discuss his new job. He apologized for not being at the game, said he knew I would do an amazing job and to contact him with any questions. Then he started a new text thread including the two guys from his team who are taking over this part of the project, and that was the end of our communication. It was kind of formal and stilted, and I know he's struggling, the same as I am. I know I didn't imagine our connection. But he's made his decision, and it's probably for the best. I mean, my dream career is here in Seattle, and his is in Boston. Both are demanding careers that would make it hard to balance any kind of relationship, let alone a long-distance one. And that's not even counting all the shit between his dad and mine. Fuck, maybe if I just keep repeating all the reasons it can't possibly work out, I'll start to feel better about it. I mean, it's definitely the responsible thing to do. I just fucking wish things were different. I know it's only been a few days, but the ache in my chest still feels like a gaping wound, and I don't know if I'm ever going to feel whole again.

Josie says I just need to be patient; she thinks there's more to our story. She did a tarot reading for me yesterday and came up with some woo-woo prediction that I was going to be experiencing enormous changes in all areas of my life very soon. As much as I'd like some hope to cling to, I know that's all just wishful thinking.

But this is our last game until after Christmas. The league pauses for several days over the holiday so players have time with their families. Ever since I was a little kid, my dad has always thrown a big party on Christmas Eve for anyone associated with the league who doesn't have other plans. It's usually well attended by guys from all up and down the West Coast. There are a lot of players whose families are too far away to visit for only a couple of days. Or there are some players who don't want to make the trip and fuck up their sleep routines, et cetera. But it's only a three-hour flight from LA to Seattle, and they don't have to worry about time zone changes, so anyone who's around often comes into town to celebrate.

Dad always offers to have guys sleep at their place, but he also books a block of hotel rooms at a nice hotel not far from their house. He takes care of everything, including making sure the travel expenses are all covered for any team staff that might not have other plans, the guys who don't make the big bucks that players do. My mom even makes sure everyone who attends gets a gift, and she does research for months to get gifts for everyone who might come. It's especially nice for younger players from overseas who might not know a lot of people yet. It's just another way my dad has always shown that he's a good person underneath all of his toxic masculinity bullshit.

The party is always fun. It's a nice tradition and I would have loved to bring Ben, but I'm sure he'll be with his family. I hope his stepdad is doing well; I'm sure holidays are stressful if you have a parent in a care facility. But Josie will be coming, of course, and since Brad's already in town since the Sasquatch are playing his Florida Jaguars tonight, he's staying, even though the rest of his team is flying back to Florida after the game. My other brother Mike will come into town tomorrow after his LA Icons play their last pre-Christmas game. Mom said something about him possibly bringing a new girlfriend, so that might be interesting to watch. Chrissy will be bringing Tom, and overall, it will probably be nice for all of us to be together for the holiday.

But that's a couple of days off. Right now, I need to focus on getting through the next few hours. I've gone over everything a million times, so I think everything should go off without a hitch.

I'm at the players' bench getting some stuff organized when one of the equipment techs comes up to me. "Hey, Aleks, there's a call for you down on the landline in the locker room."

"There is?" I ask, confused. "Did they say who it is?" Nate just shrugs unhelpfully. I roll my eyes at him, and he laughs. "What, do I look like, your secretary? Go talk to them," he says good-naturedly, and I toss a towel at him as I head down the tunnel to the same phone where I took the call about Josie's car accident a couple of weeks ago. Trying not to think about that, I answer the call.

"Hello, this is Aleks Warren speaking."

"Hi, Aleks, my name is Julie. I'm Bruce Tremaine's assistant from the Boston Bears. Bruce would like to speak with you. Can you hold on just a moment?"

My brows furrow in confusion. Bruce Tremaine is the general manager for the Boston Bears. I've met him a couple of times through my dad, but never in a professional role. "Um, sure, no problem." *What the hell is this all about?*

A few minutes later, his voice comes over the line. "Heya, this Aleks?" His voice is kind and full-bodied, sort of like the man himself, from what I remember. A former NHL player, Bruce discovered his true calling as a coach after retirement. He's probably about sixty-ish, close to my dad's age, and he's heavyset, a big man who was all muscle in his youth but has added a little more padding around his middle as the years have gone by. It's been a few years since I've seen him, but I remember liking him a lot. "This is Bruce Tremaine. I think you and I have met a few times through your pop, right?"

"Hi, Bruce. I think we've met before, yeah," I say, still totally confused.

"You're probably wondering what the fuck is going on here, am I right?" He laughs, and the sound makes me want to laugh too. I can hear the smile in his voice, and if I remember right, he looks like a smaller, beard-less Santa Claus. Smiley and happy with red cheeks and sparkly blue eyes.

"Well, yeah, I guess I'm a little curious," I chuckle. "Not that I mind or anything."

"Well, Aleks, I'll be up-front with you. I don't like to play games, and I'm sure you're busy. Now, things haven't hit the press just yet, but there will be a release going out tonight after the game. We've had to let two of our assistant GMs go this afternoon. There was some shady shit going on, and they made the mistake of thinking that because I'm old, I'm also blind and dumb. Which I am not. I won't go into details, but it's not a great situation for us, and I've had to clean house. I'm hoping we've got to the root of the decay, but only time will tell. Anyway, my point is, I've been talking to your boss, Carson Wells, and he speaks very, very highly of you. He said you've been an incredible asset to the Sasquatch already, and you've got those guys down on the farm team running like a well-oiled machine."

"Oh, thanks. That's great to hear, Mr. Tremaine," I say, still wondering what the fuck is going on.

"Call me Bruce," he says before he continues. "So, as you can imagine, having to let a bunch of people go on short notice like this is a big blow to the team. There's going to be press since, like I said, these guys were involved in some shady shit. But aside from all of that, I need to get them replaced ASAP so I can keep this goddamn hockey team afloat."

I swallow. "Sure, that makes sense." *What the actual fuck?*

"So, Aleks, based on Carson's glowing reference for you and what a great job you've done with the EC Eagles, I was wondering if you'd entertain the idea of moving here to the East Coast to take a position as one of my assistant GMs."

My jaw drops open, and I let out an audible gasp, causing Bruce to bark out a loud laugh.

"I, um, but what I, uh, are you—I mean, are you serious right now?" I ask, my voice rising to a pitch just this side of hysterical.

"I am serious. I've talked with Carson, and he gave me permission to talk to you. But he wanted me to make sure to tell you that if you want to stay in Seattle with the Sasquatch, he would love to keep you, so you're under no obligation. We'll have to go through an official interview process to keep the folks in HR happy. I get the final say on who gets the job," Bruce says.

"Anyway,' he continues, "you'll be coming in as a junior person, replacing people with a lot more experience, but there is a lot of room here for you to move and grow within the Bears organization. Hell, young man, I'm not gonna live forever, and I gotta retire sometime, assuming ownership doesn't put me out to pasture before I'm ready to make the call myself." He chuckles at his self-deprecating joke. "But my point is, there are paths forward for you here that might be a little clearer than they are with the Sasquatch."

I am absolutely, completely fucking blown away. My head spins as he keeps talking about benefits and contracts and I don't even know what the fuck. *Holy fucking shit on a shingle.* I just got offered an assistant GM position. In Boston, of all places. The Bears are a storied hockey team, one of the originals. They've struggled the past few seasons, but it sounds like at least some of the reasons for that will be gone. And best of all, it's where Ben is going to be. I don't know whether that will even matter, given that the long-distance issue was only one reason for him breaking up with me, but I can't extinguish the flame of hope that starts to burn brightly inside me. Maybe there's a way after all.

"God, yes, of course, Bruce, that would be amazing. I would love to come work for the Bears!"

CHAPTER 24
Ben

"**M**erry Christmas!" my sister, Lauren, yells from the kitchen when I walk into my mom's condo. Because Bob has been doing amazingly well on the medication during the drug trial, we're able to have Christmas at my mom's condo instead of at the care home. Being able to bring him home for short trips again is something we thought was over for him. Thanks to the miracle of modern science, we've been able to get some more real, quality time with my stepdad. *That's exactly why you're moving to Boston, Benjamin. To help create more of these moments for thousands of other families.* I need to remember the big picture. I'm not moving there for me; I'm moving there for all the families like ours who my research can help and for Dennis Madsen, who keeps telling me how happy he is that he can hand over his research to me, that I'm the only person he feels confident to trust with his legacy.

I'm coming to my parents' place directly from the airport, having just flown home from two days in Boston, where I met with Dennis and the board of trustees at Boston University. It didn't take them long to make their decision, as Dennis had promised. They extended their offer to me earlier this morning. I just have to sign the paperwork and send it back, and my dream job is mine. The thing I've been working toward for my entire career.

It's going to be good. I just need to get there and get to work. It will be amazing. My parents are so goddamn proud of me it hurts my heart. My mom, while she keeps talking about how much she'll miss me, keeps cooing about how much fun she's going to have on her trips to Boston to visit. And in the last week or so, she's even been very cautiously talking about bringing Bob to Boston for a visit. The look on her face when she talks about that is almost enough to bring me to my knees. I will do anything to help my mom have a tiny piece of the life she dreamed about for so long. She deserves her piece of happiness, and being able to help make that happen is what I've wanted for my entire adult life. It's why I chose to go into medicine in the first place. *So why the fuck am I so completely and utterly miserable?*

It's December 23, otherwise known as Festivus—because my family are serious freaks about *Seinfeld*. It's ridiculous, but it's our special form of ridiculous. Lauren is on call for Christmas Eve and Christmas Day this year, so as usual, we're doing our celebration a little early. Depending on how tiring it is for Bob, I may drop by and hang out with them tomorrow and on Christmas Day, but there's just as great a chance that I'll sit home and chill out on my own. It sounds like a shit way to spend the holiday, but since I'm moving in a few weeks, there's no shortage of stuff that needs to be done. Somehow, the thought of starting to pack all my stuff into moving boxes makes me feel sick to my stomach. But it's probably just that I need to get to work on it, same as the job itself. It all feels overwhelming right now. That's probably my issue; I'm sure it's not that I feel sick when I think about not being able to see Aleks again.

As the evening progresses, I notice both my mom and Lauren sneaking weird glances at me from time to time. I'm doing my damnedest to hide the fact that I'm miserable, but my mom always knows, and my sister inherited those special antennae that tell her exactly what I'm feeling.

Lauren and I are in the kitchen cleaning up after dinner when my mom comes in, grabs a dish towel, and starts drying the pots and pans I'm washing.

"Mom, you did all the cooking. Go sit with Dad and put your feet up. Lauren and I can do this," I say, trying to nudge her out of the way.

"Oh, stop," she says, elbowing her way back to the sink. "Bob's in there snoozing in his recliner. What am I going to do, sit there and listen to him snore?"

"Mom," I start to argue, but I know this battle is lost.

"I want to talk to you anyway," she says, busting out her No-Nonsense Mom Voice. "Benjamin, it's clear there's something bothering you. You've barely cracked a smile all evening, and you've been more distracted than I've ever seen you. It can't only be about your move. What is going on?"

I look at Lauren for help, but she just lifts her shoulders in a shrug. "She's right, Ben. I thought this was literally your dream job, but you've been walking around here tonight looking like your hamster died." Lauren looks concerned too, and I hate that they're worried about me. *God, why am I such an idiot?*

"Okay, okay, fine." I hold my hands up in surrender. "You've got me." So, I sit at my mom's kitchen table and spill my guts to her and my sister, who listen intently while I talk, their faces both masks of sympathy.

"It sounds like you really care about Aleks," Mom says, and Lauren nods.

"I really do. But the whole thing is so new, and I have no way of knowing whether it will work out. And the history between Bob and Kent—I mean, god, Mom, Aleks' father is the one who ended Bob's career. And he's at least partially responsible for the brain damage he's dealing with now. I can't do that to you and Dad."

"Benjamin Jacobs, I want you to listen to me very carefully right now," Mom says in the voice I know means business. It's like steel overlaid with silk, and when she uses it, I know she's not shitting around. "If

Aleks Warren is someone who is important to you, in any way, I will not be able to live with myself if the reason you cut him out of your life is because of us."

"Oh, Mom, it's not like it's all you. I mean, his family is obviously—"

"*No*, I said *listen*," she nearly shouts, causing Lauren and me to exchange surprised looks. Lily Jacobs-Prescott is *not* a yeller. "Ben, what happened between Kent and Bob happened years ago. It should all be water under the bridge by now. Yes, what Kent did was wrong and vicious, but hockey has always been a violent game. Bob always knew he was rolling the dice. Every night, he knew there was always a chance he could get badly hurt."

"But god, Mom, Kent Warren is just such an asshole. Even now, he's still denying that CTE is even a real condition. It's just so stupid. And that's Aleks's father."

"I know, honey. But I have my suspicions that part of the reason Kent Warren is so vocal about denying CTE is because it would mean he would have to come to terms with how much damage he caused. I don't know what's in his mind, and it doesn't matter. Kent might well be an asshole, but that's not Aleks. It's his father."

Lauren shrugs. "Mom's right. Just because his dad's a prick doesn't mean he's a prick," she says. "Has Aleks given you any indication he's like that? Like, that he's a completely self-centered asshole who's only out for number one?"

"No, not at all. Aleks is incredible." I smile in spite of my misery. Thinking about what an incredible person Aleks is has that effect. "He's an amazing friend. I saw him drop everything in the middle of a Sasquatch game that was really important to his career to be with his best friend when she was in a car accident." My heart warms, remembering how frantic Aleks was when he was worried about Josie.

"There you go. Right there, that tells you he places more value on people he loves than his father does—or at least than he did back then," Mom says. "Look, honey, if you and Aleks can't work things out for other reasons, well, maybe that's the way the cookie crumbles. But I will not let you use this family as an excuse to be apart. This isn't Romeo and Juliet."

I chuckle before looking at her with amazement. "Okay, well, that's true, I guess. I mean, I don't think either of us was planning on drinking poison."

Lauren snorts.

"But you and Dad... You guys are really both fine with what happened with Kent Warren?" I ask, kind of in awe.

"You can go and ask your dad yourself once he wakes up from his post-turkey nap," she chuckles. "But I promise you, we both made our peace with everything a long time ago. Life is too short to hold grudges like that. And it's also much too short to walk away from someone you love over trivial things." She gives me a meaningful look.

She gets up from the table, squeezing my shoulders, planting a kiss on the top of my head, and pausing as she walks behind my chair. "All Bob and I have ever wanted is for you two to be happy," she says quietly. "And JJ, your father, he felt the same way, even when you were babies. He never gave one tiny rat's ass what you two would turn out to be, as long as you turned out to be happy and healthy. And he would be so proud of you both." There's a smile in her voice, and

I know she's looking at Lauren as she gives my shoulders a squeeze. Lauren and I exchange a smile, both our eyes glassy. Neither of us remembers our father, but my mom has always done a good job of keeping him alive for us, even all these years later.

"The other thing you need to know, Ben, is that if this job isn't what you want, or if it's not the right time for you to move to Boston, or you don't feel right about it for any reason, you need to know you could *never* disappoint us. We are so proud of you already, of both of you. We just want you to find happiness, and if staying here and being with Aleks brings you happiness, that's what I want for you, more than anything else." She kisses the top of my head again, and Lauren sniffles as she quickly swipes a couple of stray tears from her cheeks and nods.

"Mom's right. The most important thing is being happy. Don't take this job if you don't think it's the right thing to do," she says before walking to the sink to help Mom work on the last few dishes. I grab another dish towel, but my mom shoos me out of the kitchen.

"No, I want to finish the last couple of things. You know I like to wash my grandmother's China myself, so if it breaks I can't blame anyone else." She grins. The last couple of things left to wash are an antique gravy boat and a couple of other plates that have been in my mom's family forever.

On my way back to the living room, I see the snow falling outside has changed from big, fat snowflakes to tiny little ones, so the temperature has probably dropped, meaning the snow will stick around for a while. Bob is still snoozing in his lounger, so I throw on my coat and boots.

"I'm going to take a quick walk around the block," I call to Mom and Lauren.

When I exit their building, it's like I've entered another world. Seattle doesn't often get this fluffy, powdery, soft snow. Usually, it's the thick, wet stuff that's great for snowballs but not much else.

There aren't many people out. The way the holiday falls this year means a lot of folks have today off as well as tomorrow and Christmas Day, so the neighborhood is quiet and peaceful. The snow also means a lot of people will stay in and hibernate tonight, and we're far enough from the main shopping area of town that there aren't even any last-minute shoppers around. I pull out my phone to check the weather and feel like someone's kicked me in the gut when the photo Josie took of Aleks and me in front of his Christmas tree that afternoon pops up. *God, how was that only a week ago?* Not calling him is probably one of the most difficult things I've ever done. All I want is to feel him snuggled up against me, running his hand over my chest and making those sleepy little snuffling noises he makes when he sleeps.

The forecast has changed, and it looks like we'll be getting a big dump of the white stuff. In fact, it now says that by Christmas Day, we might be totally snowed in. Hmm. An extra-white Christmas, I guess. That'll be kind of nice.

I slide my phone back into my pocket and try to concentrate on staying in the moment. The feel of the cold, crisp air against my face, the way the snowflakes stick on my winter coat. The soft shushing sound as I trudge through the couple of inches already on the ground. I've always liked the way snow deadens the sound of everything. I don't really believe in a higher power, but there is something sacred about a fresh snowfall.

I walk for a while, the white stuff starting to pile up at the edges of the streets. It's coming down faster now, and for a few minutes, I just breathe, liking the way the cold air feels in my nose. I stand transfixed before the streetlight, watching the snow fall.

I don't know how long I've been standing there when it hits me like a tidal wave: What am I doing? I've never felt a connection to anyone like I do to Aleks. What am I doing walking away from that? I'm not romantic enough to believe that there's someone out there for everyone. I know beyond a shadow of a doubt that *not* everyone finds a person, and fewer still find their "right" person. I know what Aleks and I have is new, and there are so many strikes against us, so many forces that will make it difficult to succeed, but what I realize, standing there under that streetlight, is that none of that matters. There's no guarantee that it will work out, but I'd be a damn fool to walk away from what we have without at least trying.

I turn and jog back to Mom's condo quickly, not wanting to waste time; I have plans to make. I chuckle, thinking of the old movie *When Harry Met Sally*. There's a line in there at the end, when Harry's racing across the city on New Year's Eve to tell Sally he loves her, that's always stuck with me. It's something about realizing that when you figure out you want to spend the rest of your life with someone, you want the rest of your life to start right away, and that's exactly how I'm feeling. I don't know how I'm going to make it happen, but I'm going to find a way for Aleks and me to be together.

After a quick goodbye to my family, I head home. I've made the decision to try and get Aleks back, but truthfully, I don't have a plan for how that's going to happen yet. I know I want to do something special, something that will make it clear how serious I am about him. I haven't returned the Boston University paperwork yet. I can still stay here in Seattle with Aleks, and if that's what it takes, I'm going to do it.

I haven't been home too long when my phone rings, a number I don't recognize coming up on the screen.

"Hello, this is Ben," I answer.

"Ben Jacobs. This is Kent Warren calling," says the voice, and I nearly drop my phone in shock.

"Kent... Ah... Hello..."

"Hi, Ben," he says, sounding strangely nervous. "Look, ah, I'm sure you're wondering why I'm calling you, so I'll get to the point. I owe you an apology. I had a conversation with my son, and, um, I've been doing some thinking." Kent clears his throat. Meanwhile, I'm still too surprised to do anything more than grunt in response. "I should never have stuck my nose where it didn't belong and tried to stop your helmet safety project. That, ah... that was not appropriate. I was letting my personal feelings get involved. It wasn't my place to interfere, and I'm very sorry. For what it's worth, I've already spoken with Carson Wells and apologized to him also. And I mentioned I spoke to Aleks too. I won't be in your way any longer with your project."

"Oh," I said, still stunned but thankful I'd recovered enough by that point to at least acknowledge the man. "I, um... This is a surprise, Kent, but thank you for the apology. I appreciate that."

He clears his throat before continuing. "Good. Well, ah, there's more. Um. So, Aleks told me that you two have been seeing each other, and, well, he didn't give me any details or anything, but he said you and he were, um, that you had decided it would be better to... not continue your relationship, and part of that reason is my fault." He pauses. "I'm so sorry about that. Truly. I just want what's best for my son, even though my behavior hasn't really shown that. But, um, I'm getting a little off track here. I wanted to tell you I just spoke with your stepdad for the first time in a very long time."

"What?" My jaw drops. He was just talking to Bob? He must have called right after I left. *Holy shit.*

"Yeah. I can understand your surprise." His chuckle is self-deprecating. "But your stepfather was unbelievably gracious. He was much kinder than I deserve after my behavior for all these years." Kent's voice sounds grave now, and he sniffles, clearly emotional.

"Wow. Well, Bob's a good man. I'm glad you were able to speak to him."

"I'm very glad and so grateful he would even take my call. Um, but anyway, Bob and Lily are going to come to our house tomorrow for brunch. Elaina, my wife, is very excited to see them both again. And then, I'm having a gathering of NHL people. It's an annual

Christmas party thing, and I was hoping you might join us since you're working so hard to make the game safer for everyone. And, well, Aleks will be here also."

Suddenly, I know exactly how I'm going to show Aleks how much he means to me. "Yeah, Kent, thank you. I'd love to come to the Christmas party."

CHAPTER 25
Ben

Christmas Eve dawns bright and sunny. It's cold and crisp, and with the snow already on the ground, the sunshine is blinding. It's unusually cold for Seattle, still not warm enough for the snow to melt, so we haven't entered that icky, slushy phase where there's no way to step outside without getting wet feet. I called my parents after speaking to Kent Warren last night, and sure enough, they said they were planning to have brunch with the Warrens and to stay for the first little bit of the party so Bob could see some of his old friends but would probably leave early. My parents asked if I wanted to join them for brunch, but I decided that would be better as a more private gathering. It seemed like Kent might have more he wants to say to Bob.

I'm nervous as fuck, but I asked Declan to come with me to the party for moral support. Fortunately, he was available since it appears his new relationship with Chloe may have burned itself out, although I'll need to talk to him about that when I can concentrate better.

As we pull up to the spacious mansion overlooking Lake Washington, golden light spills out the windows, and the place looks like something out of a movie, with a thirty-foot tall noble fir tree adorned with white twinkle lights and elegant red bows standing tall next to the winding driveway.

Walking inside, Dec and I are both bowled over by how beautiful it is. It feels like it's on par with a tech billionaire's mansion. "Whoa, this is something else," I murmur to Dec, whose eyes are wide as he takes everything in.

"Yeah, no shit. I knew Warren did well with investments after he retired, but holy shit. This place is incredible."

There are a lot of people here already, and everyone is dressed casually in jeans and maybe the odd pair of khakis. It's a sharp contrast to the formality of the décor, but it's kind of nice. Like you can admire the stunning home and its décor, but you can be relaxed and comfortable as you're doing it. It makes the house and the people seem more accessible and real. I wonder if Aleks likes this annual tradition.

To the right of the entryway, the two-story great room has floor-to-ceiling glass doors that open out onto an enormous back deck, where heat lamps are keeping the temperature comfortable enough that people can step outside for a breath of fresh air and check out the gorgeous view of moonlight shimmering across the lake. Another massive tree trimmed with intricate crystal ornaments that catch the light is the focal point of the big room, and I spot several current NHL stars already gathered with drinks in hand. A huge river-rock fireplace flanked by built-in bookcases takes up one whole wall, and the firelight spills out into the room, casting a warm and friendly glow.

The sweeping grand staircase is draped with garlands of fragrant fir and more twinkling lights. Dec and I make our way downstairs to a media room, where classic NHL game footage plays across a cinema-sized screen. I spot several current rookies, most of them young guys from Europe, battling it out at pool and foosball tables. Laughter and the sounds of Christmas music echo off the dark wood-beamed ceilings down here, and there's another terrace off this room, complete with more heat lamps that create enough warmth that people can sit outside in cozy lounge chairs, complete with soft blankets perfect for cuddling underneath. This room sports another beautiful tree, this one decorated with red and gold ornaments, and the whole effect is stunning.

Declan and I circulate for a while, but I'm starting to get restless as I haven't spotted Aleks yet. But I'm assuming Kent would have said something to me if he wasn't going to be here, as he knows what I have planned for a bit later.

We spot my parents, who are happy to see Declan since it's been a while, and Dec is blown away at how much better Bob looks. It makes me feel good that it's not just us who's noticing the big difference his new medication seems to be making. It's fucking wonderful. My heart clenches, and even though I know being with Aleks is what I want more than anything in the world, I hope we can figure out a way for me to take over the Boston University lab. It's almost like a miracle, watching how much science has helped my dad. I fucking love it.

Suddenly, I spot Aleks talking to some Sasquatch players beside the tree, and my heart leaps in my chest. He looks amazing. He's wearing those skinny black jeans of his, paired with a bright red turtleneck sweater. His green eyes sparkle like diamonds behind his black glasses, and it's all I can do not to run over and jump him right here in front of everyone.

Now that I know he's here though, my nerves are starting to kick in. Dec offers to lead me through some of my deep breathing exercises, but strangely, my nerves aren't as terrible as they usually are. I'm about to make an incredibly personal speech in front of who knows how many dozens of people, but my anxiety is surprisingly manageable.

It's not too long later when Kent comes to find me, his eyes twinkling. He asks everyone to gather around the big tree upstairs as it's time for gifts, and he sends Declan and me up to find Aleks' mom, Elaina, who's setting up the gift area in front of the tree. She gives me a genuine smile when she sees me, giving me a huge hug that helps tremendously with my nerves. "Ben

Jacobs, I remember you as a little boy." She smiles. "You've grown into such an admirable man. Aleks has been talking about you. I know he'll be so happy you're here." She gives me a wink as she bustles around getting a few more things organized. Kent appears a minute later, and I stand just out of sight of everyone in the room, almost behind the big tree. Aleks is standing off to one side, a lopsided smile on his face as he watches his dad thank everyone for coming and make a few quick jokes. But his expression turns to confusion when his dad looks over his shoulder at me and gestures for me to come out of my hiding place.

"So, just one more quick thing before we get to all the good stuff, which means, of course, before we get to the gifts," he laughs. "We have someone special here tonight—I mean, aside from Santa Claus, of course, who will be making his appearance shortly." Kent grins. "Some of you meatheads probably know of Dr. Ben Jacobs since he's been researching head injuries and ways to make our game safer for a while now." He clears his throat, eyes darting to me with a tentative smile. "But you might not know that Dr. Ben is also the son of the legendary Bob Prescott, who is also here tonight." There are a few back slaps and cheers for Bob, something that brings a smile to my face, even with nerves swamping me. "Anyway, Ben wants to say a couple of words," Kent says, and he gestures me over.

I don't know most of the guys in the room, only the ones from the Sasquatch and a couple of old friends of Bob's. I'm not sure if that makes me feel better or worse, but whatever, I'm not turning back now. Taking a deep breath, I step up beside Kent, who slaps me on the back and leans over, whispering into my ear, "Good luck, son, and thank you for everything,"

"Um, hi, everyone," I start. "I won't take up too much time here since I know you're all excited to get to the gifting part of tonight's program." I grin, and there are a few whoops from the younger guys while most people stand there staring at me politely, wondering what the actual fuck I'm doing. *Jesus, this is uncomfortable.*

"So, um, the reason I'm here tonight is because I need to apologize to someone, and I wanted to do it publicly so he knows how much I mean it. He knows how much I hate public speaking." A few polite ripples of laughter move through the room as I turn to Aleks.

"Aleks, when we first met and I figured out who your dad is, I told myself a story about you that was completely untrue. And even when I got to know you, part of me still clung to that idiotic story. I was so invested in that lie I allowed it to force me into making a dumb decision that tore us apart.

"Part of the reason I kept lying to myself about you was because I was scared of what it would mean if I didn't. If I kept telling myself that you were someone you're not, I wouldn't have to face how much you mean to me. Because that was scary as shit." I chuckle self-consciously. When I look up, Aleks has moved closer to me, chewing on his bottom lip nervously.

"I told myself something that happened a long time ago mattered more than the here and now. And I stupidly believed my family would want me to choose their past anger and hurt over my feelings for you, and that was another twisted lie. I'm so sorry, Aleks. I'm so sorry it took me so long to see how important you are to me. I promise you, I will never make such a stupid mistake ever again."

His bright green eyes are shining with tears, and I have to swallow the lump in my own throat before continuing.

"So, I need you to know I'm not going anywhere. Not unless it's with you. No job is as important to me as you are. And you're my person, Aleks. You're mine, and I'm yours, and as long as you'll let me, I'll follow you anywhere."

The guys gathered around us are quiet, everyone waiting for Aleks' response. My heart nearly beats through my chest as I hold my breath, hoping I haven't royally fucked everything up and that he'll take me back and give me a second chance.

Then, in one swift motion, he closes the distance between us and tackles me. I almost don't have a chance to open my arms to catch him in time, but he wraps himself around me like a koala and crushes his mouth onto mine in a kiss that makes my knees go weak.

The guys break out into wolf whistles and hollers around us, and when we finally break apart, his face is lit up with the most amazing smile I've ever seen. "How could you even doubt that I would want you back? Of course I want you back!" His eyes are twinkling, and I can't resist kissing him again, only breaking apart when someone lets out a loud wolf whistle and several guys start hollering for us to "Get a room!"

I tense, hoping that we're not going to encounter any homophobic bullshit here of all places, although I knew there was a chance. But when I look around, all I see are smiling, happy faces.

"Alright, everyone, it's present time!" Kent shouts just as one of the biggest defensemen on the Seattle Sasquatch, Gino Santucci, comes around the corner wearing the best Santa suit I've ever seen. The only reason I know who he is is because of his incredible eye color and thick dark lashes, making him look like he's wearing heavy eyeliner and mascara when he isn't.

"Ho ho ho!" he shouts. "Merry Christmas! Now, who wants to come on over here and sit on Santa's lap?"

More good-natured laughter and shouting follow as everyone swings into the next phase of the party, leaving Aleks and me alone off to the side of the room. He grabs my hand and leads me out the french doors to the patio outside, pulling us into a less visible spot for a moment alone.

"Thank you for giving me a second chance," I whisper, pulling him close again. "I promise I'll never fuck up like that again."

He laughs, smiling like the cat that ate the canary. "Oh, I know you won't, Dr. Jacobs," he says with a huge smile. "Because I have news for you. I got offered a job—in Boston! I'm moving to Boston too!" He's literally bouncing with excitement.

"What?" I gasp. "What do you mean? How? What job?"

Aleks giggles. "I got this crazy call from Bruce Tremaine, the GM for the Boston Bears, a couple of days ago. He offered me an assistant GM position to replace one of those assholes he just had to fire because of the scandal."

The whole hockey world knows about the scandal that they've been dealing with in Boston for the last few days. Hell, they had to fire a huge chunk of their coaching and management staff.

"Holy shit on a rope! Are you serious right now?" I'm laughing, but it feels almost like hysteria because I can't believe what I'm hearing.

"Totally serious! It's not a completely done deal yet. It all has to go through HR and stuff, but he wants me to have the job, Ben! I'm going to be an assistant GM for the Boston Bears!"

"Oh my fucking god, that is absolutely amazing!" I lift him up, spinning him around as we both laugh. "I can't believe this. I'm so happy!" I breathe, finally setting him back down onto his feet. "But I meant what I said, you know. I really will follow you wherever you go, always. As long as you'll let me, I'll be here for you, I promise," I say seriously.

"I know," he replies.

Looking down at him, I can't hold it back any longer. This man is it for me. "I love you, Aleks," I whisper.

His eyes grow round, and he sucks in a short breath before breaking into another enormous smile. "I love you too, Ben."

We stare at each other goofily for a few seconds before I cover his mouth with mine again, and this time, it tastes like forever.

CHAPTER 26
Epilogue

Eight Months Later

Ben

"Honey, I'm home," I yell, walking through the front door and dropping my messenger bag on the entryway bench. I still get a little thrill every day when I get home and can yell it out, cliché though it might be. It's late July in Boston, so it's hot as fuck and muggy as a swamp outside, but I can't imagine being any happier than I am.

The hockey season ended just over a month ago, and the Sasquatch, to everyone's complete and utter shock, won the Stanley Cup. It's unheard of for a team to win the cup during its inaugural season. It's incredible and a testament to the group of players and staff that Carson Wells brought together in Seattle. Aleks and both watched the final game in utter shock, and when the Sasquatch scored the winning goal in overtime, we both freaked out and danced around our living room like we'd won the cup ourselves.

The Boston Bears didn't have quite the same level of success. After the scandal that led to Aleks getting his new job, their team morale took a big hit. A few key staff members decided to move on after it happened, and several players requested to be traded to other teams. But Bruce Tremaine, Aleks's boss, is relentlessly positive, and he vows the Bears will be a playoff team again within the next three years.

Aleks loves his new job, and he's taken to it like a fish takes to water. I swear, the man was born to be the general manager of a hockey team. Bruce has been both shocked and delighted with Aleks's insight and talent. During the short time we've been in the off-season, he's already persuaded two big-name, free agent players to join the Bears, even with all their scandal and struggle over the past few seasons. Aleks believes so strongly in the team, and in Bruce and the culture they're trying to build, his enthusiasm naturally sells it. He's even developed a close working relationship with Carson Wells, who's acting as kind of a mentor for him. Even though Bruce is from the old guard, he's very open to advice from Carson on the best way to build a new and better team culture, and together, Bruce and Aleks are working to make the Bears into a new, East Coast version of what Carson has created in Seattle. It's fun and exciting to watch the changes to take place. I couldn't be more proud of him if I tried. He's going to have a very long and successful career, and I'm thrilled I get to be at his side while he does it.

Walking into our kitchen, I find my beautiful man taking something out of the oven that smells suspiciously like my favorite chocolate chip cookies. During his off-season, Aleks has been learning to bake, and I can't say being his guinea pig has been a hardship. After we moved to Boston, it became pretty clear to both of us that our new jobs were a lot more sedentary than our old ones, so Aleks decided to revamp our diets in an effort to help us stay (or, in my case, get) healthy. He's had some hits and misses in the nutrition department, but he's gotten to be great friends with the personal chef for several of the team's players, and he's improving fast.

I slide up behind him while he's testing the cookies for doneness, wrapping my arms around his waist while pressing a long, hot kiss to the back of his neck. "Hey, sexy," I murmur when he melts back into me, leaning his head back so it rests on my shoulder and exposing his neck to me for more kisses.

"Mmmm, hi there," he replies, turning his head so I can take his mouth in a kiss. Surprisingly, living together hasn't diminished our hunger for each other at all. I don't know if it's just us or if spending so many nights apart during hockey season keeps our physical relationship scorching hot. Whatever the reason, I am not complaining.

Bruce decided Aleks should travel with the team for the end of last season, and he'll probably do it again for this upcoming full season. It's a lot of time apart; he could be away for around a hundred and fifty nights this year. It's not perfect, but we're making it work. I was surprised at how much I miss him when he's away. I've always been an introvert, and I always thought living with another person would lead me to crave time on my own. But when my desire to have Aleks close to me didn't diminish at all over the course of the final six months of the hockey season, I took it as another sign that this relationship is it for me.

I recognize that our relationship has moved fast, but I'm working hard on letting go of my fear of letting others down. My instinct to keep everyone happy nearly led to me losing out on the most important person in my life, and I'm never going to make that mistake again.

Letting my hands slide up underneath the front of his T-shirt, I take his earlobe into my mouth, giving it a gentle bite and letting my breath ghost across the shell of his ear. He shivers against me with his desire, and glancing down, I can't prevent the smirk on my face as I notice his athletic shorts have developed an obvious tent in the front.

"Mmmm. I hope your mouth isn't making promises your ass can't keep," he says with a saucy grin, and I pinch one of his nipples hard in response, laughing when he squeals and holding him tightly when he tries to squirm out of my arms.

"Hmm, I think it's you who needs to be careful," I smirk before he spins in my arms and turns to face me, snagging one of the warm cookies off the baking sheet on the way.

"Open," he commands, and I immediately do as he asks, causing his eyes to darken as he breaks it in half and feeds me the gooey, warm cookie. Before he pulls his hand away, I lean in and capture his chocolate-covered fingers, sucking each one of them clean while never breaking our eye contact.

By the time I'm finished, he's panting, and the second I release his last finger from my hot mouth, he's on me, pushing me backward across our kitchen until I'm pressed up against the wall, where he then lunges at me, jumping into my arms and wrapping his legs around my waist and claiming my mouth like it's the last thing he'll ever do.

God, I love this. Our dynamic is filled with so much push and pull it's never the same twice, and I love it. As much as I'm a caretaker at my very core, with a deep longing to protect and care for him, I trust him so much that I let him take care of me too, and that's something I've never shared with anyone before.

Breaking our kiss so I can take a breath, I catch his eyes. "You know, this wasn't actually my intention when I came in here, but you're just so fucking irresistible I can't control myself," I laugh.

Aleks raises an eyebrow and wiggles against me, rubbing our cocks together through our clothes and pulling a groan out of me. "I like you out of control," he says, looking up at me through his eyelashes. "The perfect, calm, composed Dr. Jacobs going absolutely wild for me is one of my favorite things."

"Well, you should know that if I get you upstairs into our bed, I don't think we're coming back down here for a long, long time, so you might want to make sure everything's turned off in here."

He grins and moves to put his feet on the floor, but not before he leans in and nips my bottom lip. "Give me two minutes, and I'll meet you upstairs." He punctuates his statement by cupping my dick through the material of my pants, giving me a firm squeeze before he turns back to the oven.

"Don't be long," I growl before turning to head up to our bedroom.

I couldn't have imagined a more perfect life for myself if I tried. I love what Aleks and I have and the best part is, we're only just getting started. I can't wait for the puck to drop on a new season.

Thank you for reading The Night Before!

Want more Seattle Sasquatch?
Rylan: Seattle Sasquatch Book 1, is available December 26, 2024
Find it here:
https://mybook.to/rylan
Or learn more at www.harperrobson.com

Up Next from Harper Robson
December 26, 2024

The Seattle Sasquatch: M/M Hockey Romance

The Seattle Sasquatch took the NHL by storm, shocking the hockey world by winning the Stanley Cup in their inaugural season. But just a couple of years later, the team is grappling with the pressure of staying on top in a cutthroat league. As egos clash and tensions reach a boiling point, their once-unbreakable bonds are put to the ultimate test.

At the heart of the storm is team captain Rylan Collings, who led the Sasquatch to their first heart-stopping championship, but is now haunted by his own personal demons and carries the weight of his team's struggles on his shoulders.

In net, Louis Tremblay, the cheeky, mischievous goaltender, must contend with a younger hotshot who's gunning for the number one job.

Other players, their new Coach, and General Manager Carson Wells must all navigate their own struggles and wrestle with secrets, all while trying to lead this talented but troubled team back to the summit of the hockey world.

Will the Sasquatch buckle under the pressure, leaving team ownership with no choice but to break up their beloved squad? Or will they find the resilience to conquer personal demons, defy expectations, and hoist the Cup again?

Each book in the series is a steamy, standalone romance.

Rylan: Seattle Sasquatch Book 1

December 26, 2024

https://mybook.to/rylan

Rylan Collings, veteran superstar and team captain of the Seattle Sasquatch, is struggling. After stunning the hockey world and winning the Stanley Cup in their inaugural season, they've dropped to the basement of the standings, and Rylan carries the responsibility on his shoulders. Burdened by personal demons and the weight of leadership, his world is turned upside down when Jamie Pirelli, a cocky young hotshot with a questionable reputation joins the team, threatening the team's fragile chemistry.

As tensions rise both on and off the ice, Rylan must confront his past and navigate unexpected feelings if he hopes to lead the Sasquatch back to greatness.

Rylan is a steamy, hurt-comfort M/M Hockey Romance. Seattle Sasquatch Book One.

Pre-Order it today at https://mybook.to/rylan

Sign Up for Harper's Newsletter for all the updates on the Sasquatch.

https://www.subscribepage.com/harperbackmatter

All My Thanks

Thanks so much for reading *The Night Before.* Writing Ben and Aleks' story was fun, although it was probably the most disorganized writing project I've ever tackled. My biggest thanks are to my amazing editors, Sandra and Julia from *One Love Editing.* I don't know how their magic works, but I'm incredibly grateful for it. Please know that any mistakes left in this book are 100% my fault, probably because I missed something Sandra or Julia told me about more than once!

My oldest bestie, Carrie B is always at the top of my list of people to thank. Never doubt how much I love you and appreciate you, my sister from another mister!

This year, because of our family's move to San Diego, I've been able to get to know an old friend even better. Shannon C. was the first person in my real-life I told about my books. I'll never forget how encouraging you were then, and still are today. Thank you so much, Shan.

One of the things no one tells you when you're growing up is how hard it can be to make new friends once you're older. This year I was lucky enough to make an amazing new friend who happens to be one of the kindest, most encouraging people I've ever met. She also happens to be an incredible writer. Duckie Mack, I'm so happy our paths crossed!

Cate Ashwood, from Ashwood Designs, produced a wonderful cover for this book, as she always does. Thank you so much, Cate!

And, as usual, thank you to everyone who has read any of my books! It still shocks me that people actually want to hear about these characters that run around inside my head. I'm so happy I get to keep working at this writing thing.

I have big plans for 2024, so stay tuned. You can join my newsletter at harperrobson.com or you can email me anytime at harper@harperrobson.com. I love hearing from you!

Love & light,

Harper
December, 2023

Also By Harper Robson

A Clean Slate(Available for free at www.harperrobs on.com)

An Unexpected Gift: A Hot Dam Homes Christmas Novella

The Seattle Sasquatch Series

Rylan: Book 1

December 26, 2024

Louis: Book 2

Coming in Spring, 2025

Austin: Book 3

Coming in 2025

Carson: Book 4

Coming in 2025

Part of the *Seattle Sasquatch* World

The Night Before: Aleks & Ben

All books are available on Amazon and in Kindle Unlimited (unless otherwise noted)

Get To Know Harper

Harper Robson grew up dreaming about being a writer someday. That someday didn't arrive until she was in her mid-forties–but better late than never! While traveling that long and winding road, she worked in marketing, software development, the oil & gas industry and spent more than a decade as a stay-home mom. She grew up in Vancouver, BC, but feels most at home in the leafy green suburbs of Seattle, Washington. In 2023 Harper and her clan pulled up stakes and headed south to live in San Diego, California. She was sure she'd miss the rainy, gray days of the Pacific Northwest, but it turns out regular doses of sunshine and palm trees are pretty easy to get used to, and San Diego feels more like home every day.

She's a mom to two teenaged boys and an adorable but slightly naughty yellow Labrador Retriever. Her husband works in the tech industry and he makes her laugh every single day.

A true PNW girl, Harper loves the rain but is always planning her next beach vacation. Her favorite things include road trips, classic rock, the Seattle Kraken, her dogs and drinking champagne for no reason at all.

She would love to hear from you anytime! Email her at harper@harperrobson.com and sign up for her newsletter at https://subscribepage.com/harper-backmatter

Let's Connect

The best way to keep up with all things Harper is to sign up for the VIP Newsletter

https://www.subscribepage.com/harpernewsletter

Facebook: Harper Robson
Join My Facebook Group: Harper's Heartbreakers:
https://www.facebook.com/groups/harpersheart-
breakers
Instagram: @harperrobsonauthor
TikTok: @harperrobsonauthor
BookBub: @harperrobsonauthor

Goodreads:

https://www.goodreads.com/author/show/22284469.Harper_Robson

Amazon Author Page
authors.amazon.com/harperrobson

Website: www.harperrobson.com
Visit shop.harperrobson.com for great prices on audiobooks, signed paperbacks and more!

Get Your Free Book
A Clean Slate

Head over to

www.subscribepage.com/harperbackmatter
to sign up for my VIP newsletter. You'll receive a
free copy of *A Clean Slate*, Eric and Drew's steamy,
age-gap love story.

Eric

I've been dealing with a chronic illness since I was
nine years old, and, believe me, it's a drag. Being a
Type 1 diabetic affects every relationship in my life,
from my parents all the way through the guys I date.
After getting unceremoniously dumped because of it,
I've decided that romantic relationships aren't in the
cards for me. The last thing I want is to be a burden

on anyone. But when my best friend drags me to a weekend memorial for his grandmother and I meet his uncle, I start to wonder if he means it when he tells me I could never be a burden.

Drew

Being a single, gay man in New York city and making a decent living as a writer isn't a bad gig. But after the end of a long-term relationship, I'm at a crossroads. I can stay here and continue on with life as I know it, or I can take this opportunity to make a big change and start over in a new place. I've spent my entire adult life resisting change, but when I travel across the country for my mother's memorial weekend, I meet someone who makes me think that jumping in with both feet might not be the worst decision. The problem is, he's my nephew's best friend, and he's half my age.

A Clean Slate is a steamy, age-gap romance featuring a New York City-based writer and a West Coast Ph.D student who probably shouldn't fit together, but somehow do.

Made in the USA
Middletown, DE
26 October 2024